ALIEN HERO'S CLAIMED BRIDE

DRACONIAN WARRIORS BOOK 4

JUNO WELLS

CONTENTS

FOREWORD

Alien Hero's Claimed Bride is a stand-alone but is part of the Draconian Warrior's Series.

You'll enjoy it more if you start at the beginning!

Alien Warrior's Captive Bride

PROLOGUE

Many thousands of years ago, deep in the Exion star system, the first Draconian female entered the cave of ascension. She passed through the softly glowing waters, noticing tiny glowing blobs moving about. Whether they were finless fish or worms was difficult to tell, for they had the characteristics of both as well as thin filaments growing out of their frail bodies.

Knowing the cave must be her divine destiny, she forced herself to submit to the will of the gods and walked slowly through the glowing waters, emerging a queen on the other side. Her people were equal parts awed and terrified when she disappeared beneath the eerie luminescent liquid, for none had dared to pass through the glowing waters before.

Taking her rightful place as the leader of her people, all was well for a brief time. Soon her sleep became restless. A suspicion crept forward from the back of her mind, even as she felt something strange growing in her body. It moved around and playfully tickled her insides. Since she had no fever, nor evidence of disease upon her skin, horns, or wings, the healers assured her that all was well.

Then the nightmares started, and she never knew a moment's peace thereafter. Every day was a struggle to shut out the dark voice growing ever stronger in her mind. Once the symbiont took full control of her faculties, the young woman was forced to stand idly by while the creature wreaked havoc on her people.

From that day to this, every Draconian female had been forced to walk through the cave of ascension, thus becoming a queen in her own right. Those who failed to ascend were killed or sold into slavery. Death was preferable, since a Draconian female slave could look forward to lifetime of torture by beings who were furious with their treatment at the hands of the Draconian empire.

A millennium slipped idly by while the evil of the cave fell into myth. Ascension came to be known as a coming-of-age ceremony for young females, and the Draconians were taught to love this sacred right, thus perpetuating the age of the symbiont. The first symbiont was long lived and few knew it still wandered the 'verse looking for plunder and warriors.

As the decades flew by the queens grew discontent, fighting amongst themselves and battling with each other over warriors. They seemed to grow stronger, crave chaos, and feed off the misery of others. Little did the Draconians know, but the luminescent creatures floating in the waters of the cave of ascension were not some strange anomaly naturally occurring on their planet, but rather the spawn of a soul-sucker that had been driven from a nearby world.

Meanwhile on Earth, the environment was deteriorating, turning the oceans into putrid acidic cesspools devoid of all lifeforms. The lives of many males were lost in an effort to clean up the contamination, and then the worst-case scenario came to pass: a new pathogen emerged and locked onto the male genome. It took time to develop an antigen, costing more lives still. By the time it was said and done, the ratio of males to females was seriously unbalanced, with four females to every male.

Just when humans were losing all hope of survival on their harsh world, aliens made contact with the peoples of Earth. They not only offered to help manage the environmental disaster, but also provided much-needed medical supplies and foodstuffs. In return, the aliens requested the one thing Earth had in surplus.

Voluntary human brides were offered in exchange for the supplies. Many women were all too happy to relocate to a pristine new planet with an accommodating alien husband. It beat the alternative, which was living in huge crowded bio-domes.

This is the story of first contact between a human woman and a race of ancient warriors with dragon genetic matter mixed into their biology. Cassandra will do anything to escape the alien amphibians that abducted her and avoid the auction block. Mathadar will go to any lengths to protect the frail human queen he's becoming ever more enamored with.

1 UNDER PENALTY OF DEATH

MATHADAR

Standing before a Draconian queen always made Mathadar feel like he was straddling the line between life and death. The raw power they wielded was nothing short of breathtaking. Males lived and died according to their whims. Too many of his brethren had been struck down in the prime of their lives by a queen displeased with their service to leave him feeling anything but anxious in a queen's presence.

Mathadar had no intention of joining their ranks. His family line had slowly been disposed of during the course of his lifetime, leaving only the relationships he'd forged with other warriors to comfort him. His sire was killed in battle for a planet his queen promptly blew up in order to harvest its rich mineral deposits. Such spectacular waste of life was common. In this sector of space warriors historically had a prodigious death rate.

Once Mathadar had enjoyed the company of ten brother spawn, but now they were either dead or scattered across the galaxy in the service of other queens. If any survived to this day, they'd be unlikely to ever set eyes on each other again, no matter how much he longed to look into their familiar faces. That would never happen. It haunted him to think what kind of pain they might be enduring if any had been unlucky to draw the notice of a queen.

Tucking his wings tightly behind his massive frame, Mathadar stood perfectly still as his queen stalked down the line of warriors. Inspections were designed to test a warrior's fortitude. It was unnerving for a good reason. Once a queen's eye landed on you, pain always followed.

Normally Mathadar consoled himself with the fact that his austerity ensured he was unlikely to be noticed among the many. Today was a different situation. Since he'd been tasked with leading this mission, overlooking him was not a mistake their queen was likely to make.

The huge queen slowed to a stop in front of him, crinkling her brow as if she could hardly believe that she'd cycled through so many warriors that she was now forced to utilize commanders with so little promise. It was true that Mathadar had led few missions and none of note. This was his chance to prove his worth and they both knew it.

Her hand came up to wrap around one of his tender horns. Steeling himself against her touch, the proud warrior schooled his expression into a blank stare even as her grip tightened to the point of intense pain.

Never make eye contact with a queen if you wish to live. His father's quietly whispered words snaked through Mathadar's mind even as she slowly pulled him forward.

Watching his brethren struck down by her massive claws one after another over his lifetime successfully drove home the reality that a warrior's life was of little importance to a queen. The truth of it showed clearly in her contemptuous expression. One of the massive claws sitting atop her wrists could easily slit his throat if he made a wrong move.

Though she'd gone through dozens of fine warriors in the last few lunars, she'd just stop by their home world and replenish soon. Therefore, momentary scarcity didn't enhance his value.

A male was only of value to his queen when he bred for her or risked his life to do her bidding. Since Mathadar was no breeder, his only chance at survival lay in total obedience to her will. In that, he could never fail.

Leading others into danger presented an entirely different subset of problems for him today. Sacrificing them for the success of the mission was not only standard operating procedure but an expected outcome. Unfortunately, the warriors flanking him on every side were males he knew well. He'd grown up with many of them and knew their likes and dislikes.

Having worked side by side with them and fought with them for many long solars, sacrificing them for any but the most worthy of goals was unthinkable. Then again, Mathadar wasn't being tasked with thinking. He wasn't even certain queens believed males were capable of higher reasoning or bonding to one another.

Holding back a humorless laugh, he knew their self-absorbed queen would never understand how closely males bonded to each other when they had no one else to care for. She busied herself with gowns, jewels, protocols of respect, and jostled for power and control among the other queens. Though those were her primary concerns in life, and nothing held more interest for her than securing Tarken.

When her cold glassy stare bored into his soul, Mathadar knew what she was going to do before she did it. "Mathadar, you will know pain the likes of which you cannot begin to imagine if you fail to secure my shipment. I will rend you limb from limb."

The older female had been overindulging in Tarken. Its cloying scent rolled off her in waves. That, mixed with the excess sweat the drug provoked, made her smell perfectly revolting. She was even more ruthless and unpredictable than ever now that she'd found this new addiction.

Mathadar continued to stare straight ahead, avoiding eye contact. Since her threat came in the form of a statement, he knew better than to offer a reply. This queen was lusting for another dose of the drug and therefore not interested in his reassurances. Her only desire was procuring more of the potent elixir. It seemed the life's purpose of every male aboard the ship had become a never-ending quest for more of this substance. It was becoming increasingly clear that she would stop at nothing to keep herself supplied.

Pain sliced through his attempts to remain calm under her scrutiny. One long claw dug deeply into the flesh of his shoulder. She wiggled it against his bone, barely parting the joint. Locking his jaw, Mathadar forced his body to relax. Tensing up would result in more muscles and tendons being damaged.

Her voice sounded off harshly in his ear. "You. Will. Not. Fail. Me."

Twisting slightly with each spoken word, she drove her point home. Of all the queens, this one enjoyed dealing pain more than others. She was so close he could feel the heat coming off her skin. She inhaled deeply, taking in his scent. Their queen did that a lot and it didn't make any sense. Never one to miss a good excuse to inflict damage on a warrior, she almost seemed to crave their pain. It made him wonder if she could scent his fear.

Several other warriors made muted sounds of distress and that seemed to snap her out of her desperate attempt to impress upon her commander the importance of bringing back her shipment. Her dark eyes slid away and she jerked her claw from his shoulder. So much of her behavior since becoming addicted to the elixir seemed irrational. Why maim the warrior tasked with securing her shipment right before a mission? It was almost like she couldn't stop herself.

Alarm shot through the assembled grouping of warriors when she staggered slightly as she walked away. Mathadar shook his head ever so slightly at their shocked expressions. Now was not the time to speak of what they were seeing. There would be time enough for that once the mission was completed. Mathadar was all too aware that he was tasked with holding the warriors together emotionally during this trying time as well as leading the actual mission. Their queen's odd behaviors made everything more complicated than it had to be.

The moment their sickened queen crossed the threshold and the huge bay doors closed behind her and her entourage, Mathadar motioned for the thirty assembled warriors to enter two shuttles. He'd already split them into two teams. Building in redundancies would increase the likelihood of at least one returning with the shipment their queen coveted so highly.

No sooner did he take a seat in the back of the shuttle than their medic began ripping at the arm of his uniform, attempting to heal his shoulder wound. The others were gathered in the front rows, giving them some privacy. Letting out an annoyed huff, the Draconian commander ripped his sleeve off. Though the gash was not large, it was deep.

They both knew such wounds were more exasperating and painful than serious. It took the healer only a few moments to mend the torn flesh with a healing laser. Rolling his shoulder around, Mathadar was relieved to find he'd regained full movement of the joint.

"Are you well, Commander?" Pharon looked at him with questioning eyes. They'd been friends long enough for Mathadar to know all his quirks, especially the one about not being fully confident of his healing unless there was a medical scanner to confirm the results.

Nodding, Mathadar's horns perked up. "It feels fine. Thank you, Pharon."

His longtime friend turned the medical device over in his hand, examining every tiny detail like it was new tech before reluctantly speaking to what was really bothering him. "Our queen grows ever more dependent upon the elixir, Math. You know as well as I that she cannot continue like this. We must do something."

Though he saw this coming from his medic, Mathadar's wings still jerked in aggravation. "It is not our place to question the will of a queen. To do so is a death wish. You know this, Pharon. I do not appreciate my closest friend speaking such treasonous words."

Pharon's voice dropped lower. "She doesn't even attempt to breed any longer."

When Mathadar did not respond quickly enough, Pharon pointed out the obvious. "Queens place breeding before all else. They normally have a large stable of breeders, obsess over them, and are ever on the lookout for new breeding stock. Gods of Chaos, they even sometimes resort to breeding plain warriors just for the thrill of being perverse. Our queen is not even trying to procreate."

"I have never known a queen to go twenty-nine cycles without breeding. That's almost two solar revolutions."

Lowering his voice to match that of his medic, Math continued, "We have no control over a queen. If we attempt to intervene, the other ships will converge upon us. All the queens are certain to come to her defense. Our entire crew, all nine hundred, will be obliterated. Is that what you wish?"

Jerking in his seat, Pharon fumbled, dropping his medical instrument. Recovering quickly, he reached down and snagged it from the floor. He looked the device over for damage. "You know that isn't what I want. But she also no longer visits her male offspring. Do you not find that bizarre behavior for a queen?"

Glancing around the shuttle again to see if the others were paying attention to their conversation, he discovered they were all busy with concerns of their own.

Mathadar's chest ached at the thought of her young. "I say it is a blessing that she takes no interest in her male hatchlings. Better for them if she forgets they even exist. At one time she reaped them mercilessly, ensuring only the most worthy survived."

Pharon swallowed hard, giving voice to his deepest fears. "Watching her kill off their little ones almost destroyed the breeders. I am of your mind about her lack of interest in them. It's an unexpected gift from the gods."

"It kills my soul to see her destroy one of the little ones. I will never understand the mind of a queen if I live to be a thousand." Pharon's exasperated voice lowered to a mere whisper, as if speaking his greatest fear would somehow make it come true. "I just worry that the anger of the other Draconian queens will fall heavily upon us for doing nothing to help her in her time of need. She doesn't even have a female child to groom for her replacement. When she passes, it will be as if she never existed."

Grabbing him by the arm, Mathadar hissed, "You're being morose."

"Am I? Queens live to breed other queens. It's their prime goal in life."

Mathadar was growing ever wearier of the conversation. Biting back his anger, he spat, "Why should we care about such things? Thank the gods that you and I will never see our own spawn hatched into such a troubled world." Snorting a mirthless laugh, he continued, "Though they were raised to tolerate the touch of queens from birth, our breeders are much relieved to have such a long reprieve from attending to her needs. Their little ones are safe for once and I am happy for them." Squeezing his friend's arm slightly, Mathadar added quietly, "We will do our duty by following her orders to the best of our ability. Do not worry about the future, for over that we have no control."

Pharon nodded, his horns dropping back.

Giving his shoulder another reassuring squeeze, the commander stated emphatically, "Come what may, we will endure. This is our lot in life, living on the edge, always surviving in the face of insurmountable odds."

Sucking in a shaky breath, Pharon nodded in agreement, accepting his longtime friend's wisdom. "I will be as you say, Commander."

Before Mathadar could respond, the shuttle jerked under their feet. The erratic movement interrupted their quietly spoken conversation, alerting them that they had hit the planet's atmosphere. Coming to his feet, the commander headed to the front of the shuttle to catch a preliminary glimpse of the planet as the shuttle broke through the clouds.

Mathadar suck in a breath at the sight of the awe-inspiring world that filled his vision. After the dull grays and dark shades of their ship, seeing so many living things and bright colors was a delight to his senses. If he were free to choose for himself, he'd much rather live on a planet than in space.

This particular planet was filled with thick colorful forests and dark blue oceans. As he stared at the swirling waters, Mathadar wondered why the thought of so much water made him feel uncomfortable. Though it was a beautiful sight, something threatening kicked to life in the recesses of his mind. He imagined drowning, unable to suck in oxygen as his throat is flooded with cool refreshing liquid. To have the life choked out of him by something so lovely seemed like a cruel joke from the gods.

Several of the warriors sounded off, expressing their pleasure at being allowed to land on a lush tropical world. Pharon's hand landed on his shoulder. "Whoever would have thought such a beautiful planet existed in our quadrant of space?"

Pulling away from his friend's grip, Mathadar went back to staring at the huge view screen. "The queens tolerate these worlds because they grow food and manufacture the Tarken. It's fortunate for the Balarians that they continue to ingratiate themselves in such ways, for I would hate to see such a perfect world destroyed."

Several sounded off their agreement as the shuttle landed. Once the screen went blank, they got down to business. The warriors all took a moment preparing to exit the craft, each shoving an oxygen concentrator into their nostrils. The tiny finger-sized devices sat on their upper lips, pulling in air from both ends, filtering it and concentrating the oxygen, which was pumped into their nasal cavity. The atmosphere on Balaria was light on oxygen, necessitating the use of such devices for most visiting humanoids. There was a good chance a Draconian warrior might be fine with the lighter atmosphere, but Mathadar wasn't taking any chances on their physical or mental response time being slowed by something he could easily control.

They stepped out onto the tarmac, consulted the three-dimensional maps that sprang up from the communications devices they wore on their wrists, and headed for the city square.

The remaining shuttle was scheduled to land on the opposite side of the city. Mathadar felt certain his team would be the first to secure a shipment of Tarken. Draconian warriors were naturally competitive with each other, since they were forced to be subservient to their queens. They devised a thousand different ways to show dominance amongst themselves. Such competitions were practically a national pastime among his kind.

Something about having his feet planted firmly on the ground after so many cycles in space felt strange. He allowed his wings to unfurl in a brilliant display of dominance. Feeling the gentle breeze filter around his wing base was a small pleasure he normally didn't enjoy in the confines of a spaceship. With any luck they'd be able to find the Tarken without incident and enjoy some air time before returning to the ship.

2 PAIN NEVER-ENDING

CASSANDRA

Sitting in a cold, damp cell staring at the gray slimy muck representing the sum total of nutrition she was allotted for the day, Cassandra willed herself to reach out and take the food. Forcing her hand to grasp the small clay bowl, she pulled it forward and stared down into the revolting substance. Something just under the surface moved. Her eyes grew wide. Involuntarily retching into the back of her throat, she realized the food they'd left for her was crawling with larvae of some sort. Cassandra couldn't put it back down fast enough. The clink of the clay vessel on the stone floor was a stark reminder that she would be going hungry today.

A childlike voice sounded off from the darkness. "You should eat, humon."

Squinting her eyes to peer into the dimly lit cell adjoining her own, a shadow shifted slightly. They put someone in the cell beside her during the night. She'd assumed the person was unconscious because they hadn't made a sound. Clearly she was mistaken. "It's *human,* and we don't eat things that are still wiggling."

"Entaza is supposed to wiggle. When it stops moving, you can no longer consume it."

"Oh, it has a name. Would you like to eat the Entaza? Honestly, I don't mind."

The childlike voice sounded hopeful. "I do hunger."

Cassandra shoved the small bowl nearer to the bars separating them. "You're more than welcome to it."

A small hand reached out of the shadows and a claw hooked around the edge of the bowl, pulling it forward through the bars. Sweet Jesus, it looked like an alien child's hand.

Swallowing thickly, Cassandra tried to keep her voice even. "You seem young."

There was some slurping, a slight pause, and then the girl answered. "I am fourteen turns of the seasons. Draconian females age more slowly than our males." After another pause, her young voice hardened. "I am not weak, human."

Moving forward, Cassandra grasped the bars with both hands, peering into the other cell. "I never said you were. What's a Draconian? I've never heard that term."

The alien teen snorted a laugh. "You are in Exion space. How can you not know what a Draconian is?"

"I'm in an area of space called Exion?" Shaking her head, Cassandra frowned. "How can that be? I'm from the Naxis."

"I know nothing of an area of space called the Naxis. In Exion space the Draconian queens rule. They are few, vicious, and do not tolerate other females in their territory."

Cassandra's heart froze in her chest as she tried to process this new information. If she understood the teen correctly, a limited number of alien women ruled this sector of space where no other females were permitted to live. "Is that how you ended up being a slave?"

Her fellow captive moved forward out of the shadows. Cassandra's eyes grew wide as she took in the youngster's appearance. Delicate wings peeked out on each side of her slender form, and her green skin resembled that of a reptile, with a slight variegated pattern running through it. Her nearly black eyes held just a hint of gold. Instead of hair, she had large spots and horns that were slicked back against her head. Long slender arms ended with sharp claws on three fingers and an opposable thumb. A huge talon sat atop each still-developing wrist.

"I've never seen a Draconian before. The aliens who took me are aquatics. They've kept me incapacitated. Having only a vague idea of the passage of time, I can't even say how long the voyage was or how far we traveled."

"I feel compassion for you, human, for you will not long survive the rule of the queens." The young teen rubbed her hands down the front of her tattered uniform before her eyes darted around the room. "I will suffer the same fate, but I'm determined to survive as long as possible."

Gripping the bars harder, Cassandra's mind drifted around for a solution to the girl's problem. "What of your family? Won't they be looking for you?"

She wrapped her arms around her stomach, shaking slightly. "I am unascended. No one will come for me."

Frowning, Cassandra asked, "What is 'unascended'? I don't know this word. The translator they attached to my brainstem is translating the word as 'evolved' or 'matured.'"

Wings tightening up behind her, the youngster's expression took on a forlorn expression. "My queen mother is shamed to have me as a daughter. My body rejected ascension."

Blinking at her new friend, Cassandra watched her draw into herself. Whatever ascension was, it was obviously a critical part of the coming-of-age ceremony for a teen in this girl's society. "I still don't understand."

A squeaky, annoying voice came from the doorway. "She can never follow in her queen mother's footsteps."

Seeking out the source of the statement with her eyes, Cassandra spied the tall aquatic. She was all too familiar with the wretched man. He crossed the room and stooped outside the girl's cell. Staring at her with disgust, he jerked his chin in her direction as his eyes slid over to his human captive.

"Young Draconian females must enter the cave of ascension. Whatever rituals that transpire there turn them from a female into a queen. This one failed to complete the rite successfully. There is no room in Draconian society for failed queens. Instead of being gifted with a ship and crew of their own, failed queens are killed or sold."

Cassandra turned on her captor, always ready for a chance to cut him down to size. "After years of shut-the-hell-up, you're turning out to be pretty damn chatty, Larek."

His hand flew out so fast that Cassandra scarcely had time to react. Grabbing the front of her threadbare clothing, he jerked her forward into the bars. "You never learn, do you, humon?"

Clawing smart bloody lines down his hand with her nails, Cassandra spat out, "How many times do I have to tell you to keep your hands off me, you useless sack of shit?"

Letting go of her clothing, his hand jumped to wrap around her throat before she could get away. A drop of his cold dark amphibian blood dripped onto her pale skin, drawing his notice to the trails she'd torn open on his wrist and hand. "I think we have been too lenient toward you, humon. You are a slave to the Balarians, yet you constantly harm the very hand that feeds you. Humons are not very smart, I think."

"She's a *human*, not a humon."

Cursing softly under her breath, Cassandra hated the young girl drawing their captor's attention again. "Leave her alone, Larek. She's just a kid."

Releasing her throat with a shove, he jerked slightly, making an odd squeal. Cassandra covered her ears. Balarian laughter was so high-pitched it hurt her ears. The young girl in the adjoining cell brought her wings up to cover her ears.

"Have no worry for the failed queen. Unlike you, she will be sold without a blemish of abuse. The Draconian queens are merciless, cruel, and hated in this sector of space. Many would enjoy taking out their frustrations on this failed queen. Whoever pays the most will earn that privilege of marking her first." Shooting the younger woman a quick look, he stated darkly, "Her pain will be never-ending."

The meaning of his words slowly settled over the two of them as their captor came gracefully to his feet. Staring down at Cassandra, Larek's voice turned cold. "We have barely touched you all these many solars because you are unique. I discovered the way to your world of water and even now my brethren go seeking more of your kind."

Horror bloomed in Cassandra's chest. "Stay away from Earth, you sick son of a bitch." Imagining ships filled with human women being dragged across the galaxy made her braver than she'd ever been before.

"Humans are a highly aggressive species. If you think I'm a handful, think again. Most of the women are real fighters and our males will rip you apart for daring to land on our planet uninvited."

Making the squeaking laugh again, he flipped his head happily. "Your planet now lies in ruins, humon. Earth females are ripe for the picking and pick them we will. Our people will lay waste of what is left of your world and take all that we desire."

"I'll make sure whomever you sell me to regrets the deal he makes with you. Before I'm finished no one in this sector of space will want a human woman."

Cassandra knew she was just making wild threats, threats she would follow through with in a heartbeat if she were capable. Unfortunately, it seemed that every being in the 'verse was larger and strong than a human.

His cold voice drew her from her internal musings. "Never has your kind been seen in the known universe. You are the first and therefore the most valuable."

"I doubt that. My language is in the translation program you gave me. That fact alone tells me humans are not new to this sector of space."

Squeaking out another laugh, his fins jiggled comically. "Humons are foolish creatures. You complained much when we first collected you. It wouldn't have taken us long to map your language. Luckily, humans created language programs to help your people learn each other's language. We simply matched your words with the correct language and added it our language database. After all, a dumb slave who can understand all the languages in the known 'verse is much more valuable than a smart one with no under-standing of their master's words. I've spent the last solar thinking about your likely fate and now my curiosity will be appeased."

Blinking up at him, Cassandra froze in place. It seemed the one question she most wanted to know was about to be answered. Every person wanted to know what their future held. Humans were no different. Even if death was all that awaited her, Cassandra wanted to know her fate.

"I see the worry and interest in your eyes, humon. You wish to know your fate, do you not?"

Cassandra nodded like a bobblehead doll. She was keen to hear the gruesome information that her captor seemed so eager to impart.

"Do not think for a moment that your buyer will be kinder than that of the fallen queen. Many species covet unusual female beings for pleasure slaves, breeding stock, or pets of a kind. Some fewer consider dimwitted beings such as yourself a delicacy. I care not which type of being purchases your or for what purpose. We procured you fairly and fed you all these many solars. Today is the day we get paid for all our time and trouble." He stepped back, glaring at them. "Who would have thought that two such weak and pathetic creatures would be my ticket to a better future?"

Turning on his heel, he fast walked out the makeshift door crudely built into the cave wall.

"He is a most unpleasant male. He would never survive if he were a Draconian. Some queen would have killed him long ago."

Cassandra's face contorted into a mask of fury, but her voice remained strangely calm. "Welcome to my world, kid."

"He lies about your language. I agree that your kind must be exceedingly rare but not unknown, for your language is in my translation program and I have not had a language upgrade from the Balarians. That male took great pride in his attempts to deceive us, human."

Relaxing a little, Cassandra took solace in the possibility of their being other humans in the sector. If there were humans here, she'd find them and set them free. She didn't care for being called "human" by every alien in the sector though. "My name is Cassandra Donovan."

"Why do you have two names?"

Sighing, Cassandra sucked in a deep breath before answering. "Humans like names. Most of have three names and some four or five. It's a human thing."

"I am Teladora. Draconians prefer one name, for the sake of brevity."

"I'm choosing to think of your response as an appreciation for efficiency rather than condescension."

The girl caught her off-guard with her next statement. "Now that formalities are out of the way, can we discuss escaping?"

The earnest expression on Teladora's face was evidence that she wasn't joking. Moving closer to the bars again, the older woman lowered her voice. "I've been trying to escape for years. I tried fighting the guard, pretending to be sick, and begging other beings for help. Once I got as far as an escape pod when I was on their ship. Unfortunately, nothing is keyed to accept verbal commands from a human. If you've got any good ideas, I'd love to hear them, because I'm not trying to end up on some alien's dinner plate."

"Since the Draconians are the dominant species in this quadrant of space, you are the alien," the girl pointed out blandly.

"Yeah, I'm getting that. Do you have any good ideas on getting us the hell out of here?"

"We cannot fight them. The Balarians outnumber us and are heavily armed." After a pensive moment, Teladora's expression brightened. "We must be on the lookout for Draconian males. They will battle the Balarians and secure our release."

Shaking her head, Cassandra doubted that was true.

"You mean the same warriors that sold you off in the first place?"

"I was sacrificed by a queen. Queens never leave the protection of their ship. If males are on this planet, they will do my bidding. They are honor-bound to do as I say."

Confusion creased the other woman's face. "You mean to say every Draconian male has to follow orders from a Draconian female, no matter who she is?"

Staring into her eyes, Teladora smiled impishly. "No. One of our most closely guarded secrets is our males will follow the orders of any female, not just Draconian females. All females are considered queens by our people."

"I wouldn't know about any of that, 'cause I've only seen the inside of cells like this and cages for the duration of my voyage to this area of space. God only knows how long they kept me in hyper sleep before they awakened me to slave aboard their vessel."

"It's why Draconian queens are so territorial. They are afraid an alien queen might lay claim to their warriors en-masse."

"You're giving me more hope than I've ever had that we might actually escape this hellish nightmare."

The teen turned her body slightly and fluttered her wings. "Look for males with wings like mine. Very few species are gifted with wings and fewer still with horns. These features mark us as having a dragon heritage."

Looking over her new friend uncertainly, Cassandra muttered, "Humans think dragons are creatures of myth. Are you saying that you actually turn into a dragons?"

Jerking backward slightly, the youngster frowned. "Don't be absurd. Beings don't turn into other species of beings." Leaning forward slightly, she whispered, "You might not want to say such things. It is probably why our captor believes you to be dimwitted."

"Okay, I kind of deserved that one." Grinning, she added, "Thanks for the reality check."

Still eyeing her suspiciously, the young teen nodded. "You are welcome, human."

"Please call me by my name."

The younger woman's horns drooped again. "You have a nice name. My name was to be Teladora, Queen of the *Delacroy*. The *Delacroy* is a fine training ship. I'd filled it with all my favorite warriors. Even my brothers were eager to attend me on my first foray into space aboard my own vessel."

"Not ascending must have been a real disappointment for you, going from the pinnacle of success to the bottom of the heap." Although she tried to keep her voice conversational, anger edged into Cassandra's tone slightly.

This didn't go unnoticed by her companion. When Teladora's eyes lifted there was a depth of misery almost beyond reckoning reflecting back. "You don't understand. I filled that ship with all the males I cared most about in the entire 'verse. My brothers and the rest of my crew were glad to serve me because they believed in me. They knew I would protect them. Draconian queens can be ruthless. Many enjoy inflicting pain on their warriors. I failed to ascend, so now they have been delivered into the hands of another queen, one who is probably abusing them even as we speak. It matters not to me that I failed to ascend, only that I failed to keep them safe."

"Being queen of your own ship sounds like it would have been a good life for you as well as the males you tried to save. I'm sorry it didn't go down that way." Smiling weakly, she admitted, "Teladora, Queen of the *Delacroy* does have a nice ring to it."

"Being sold into slavery makes me realize how little I value fancy names and titles bestowed for the sole purpose of giving me sovereignty over the lives of others. I can now see that such privileges should be earned. It is unlikely you are able to understand how much I am growing to hate my own name, for it was primarily chosen to make me seem important."

"Are you kidding? I hated my name growing up as well. Cassandra sounds pompous and the other kids used to tease me about being a know-it-all." Shrugging with one shoulder, she added, "As a teen, I shortened it to Cassie to fit in better." Pausing for a brief second and idea popped into her head. "'Tela' has a nice ring to it, don't you think?"

The other woman's face lit up. "Yes, it does."

Cassandra continued in a conversational tone. "Names like Cassie and Tela are less formal."

A slight smile crept onto Teladora's face. "You may call me Tela. If we are going to be uniting for a common cause and risking our lives together, we should be on intimate terms."

Cassandra laughed. "Humans consider intimacy sex."

Teladora chirped out a laugh of her own. "We are not breed-compatible, human. Therefore we will save the intimacy for the males who rescue us."

Nodding, Cassandra deadpanned right back, "Fine, but I get first choice of men if we get rescued. You aren't old enough to breed in any case."

The girl preened a bit. "Draconian queens choose their breeders at an early age. We wish to have them in place for when we come into our hormones."

"You sound like you might be intending to choose more than one male."

"Of course I wish to have a stable of breeders. Among my people, we have one queen to a thousand warriors." Laughing again, this time at Cassandra's shocked expression, Tela amended her former statement. "Naturally only a select few of those thousand males are used for breeding."

Clearing her throat, Cassandra explained, "Humans only choose a single male from the many. We're always on the lookout for our one true love, the one we consider our perfect mate."

Scrunching up her nose in a pensive expression, Teladora thought it over for a bit. "We are taught that no male is perfect. Each is to be used according to his strength. I think you should select your warrior first if you wish only one. I will happily select my stable from those who remain."

"That's real nice of you, but the males may have a thing or two to say about getting chosen by us."

Shaking her head, Teladora clarified lightly. "Most warriors have accepted that they will live their entire lives without knowing intimacies with a queen or producing offspring of their own. They are happy just to be selected for breeding."

"It makes me sad that they have no choice in mating and such a low probability of finding a mate. Imagine going your whole lifetime without experiencing sexual pleasure or having the opportunity to make a family."

Glancing away, her new friend murmured, "For the first time ever, I am sad for them as well."

Sitting face-to-face, the two women couldn't have looked more dissimilar. Cassandra's long blonde hair, pale skin, and sparkling blue eyes were a sharp contrast to

Teladora's stark, dark beauty. Yet their hearts and minds found common ground.

"You are wise for a wingless being," Tela said, breaking the quiet that had spun out between them.

"And you're smart for such a young being."

"We're really going to do this, aren't we?" Excitement strummed in the younger woman's voice.

"Escape? Hell yes, we are. First, we have to believe that we can. Then we must maintain an awareness of our surroundings and stay alert for any opportunity that presents itself."

Tela's excitement was replaced by a serious tone. "I can definitely do as you say because I have no interest in experiencing the never-ending pain our captor spoke of."

"Don't worry, we'll stick together and make it out of this mess somehow. If I can break free, I'll come for you. No matter what, you have to survive."

Tela's hands tightened on the bars and she frowned. "Do not make promises you cannot keep, human."

Forcing a grin, Cassandra shot back, "We might be small and physically weak compared to the Draconians, but humans make up for it by thinking on our feet and taking risks many other species wouldn't even consider. Just you wait and see. We'll both escape."

3 HUMAN QUEEN

MATHADAR

Wandering through the marketplace, Mathadar's team scattered to seek out purveyors of Tarken, the drug demanded by their queen. Nothing on this planet was organized or orderly. Some species were like that, but he much preferred the planets where he could make arrangements ahead of time with sellers and then simply land and conduct the transaction.

Securing a distributor for Tarken was proving to be difficult. The elixir was distilled from a rare plant found growing in the wild on some planets. It was perplexing how an advanced civilization like the Draconians could be unsuccessful in cultivating the plant.

Some scientists thought the intoxicating element was activated by natural sunlight and therefore could not be produced by the artificial light on a spaceship. Even the specimens sent to their home world were far from thriving, perhaps because of the atmosphere or different gravity. Whatever the reason, it must be secured from the worlds where it originated.

It also frustrated him that they were forced to ignore

much-needed foodstuffs and other supplies in favor of securing the precious elixir. Queens didn't concern themselves with the needs of warriors. As long as there was enough pressed food bars to keep the males energized, that was all that mattered. Because of this warriors became experts at recycling everything from water to clothing. They were even beginning to run low on parts for the ship.

Though this small planet wasn't the epicenter for trade in this sector, it did draw species from nearby worlds looking to trade. So far Mathadar has spied reptilians, synthetics, and fur-covered beings in addition to the native inhabitants, which were amphibian. He got his fair share of disagreeable looks from the other species, but none were brave enough to confront him. Since he was in uniform, he was clearly doing a queen's bidding. No one would be foolish enough to risk offending a Draconian queen.

Pharon rushed up to him looking both excited and worried. It gave Mathadar hope that he'd found the source they were looking for. Other members of his team moved forward to hear the out-of-breath medic's report. "Commander, you will not believe what I discovered in the city center."

Grasping his heaving friend by the arm to steady him, Mathadar responded, "I pray it is the Tarken we've been tasked with securing." A warning was sounding in his head, alerting him that something was amiss.

Shaking his head, Pharon's wings sprang outward in a most disgraceful display of anxiety. "They have enslaved queens. One is a fallen queen. She's so young, Mathadar, young and vulnerable. She's terrified and males are bidding on her. Word came to my ears that one failed the rite of ascension. The poor creature is fortunate to have survived this long."

"We have to do something. You know the beings of this planet will rip her apart because of their hatred for our rule over them. They will take out their frustrations with all queens on this youngling who never even became a true queen, simply because she is Draconian."

Another of his team interjected, "Perhaps we can free her, but what after that? We cannot take her aboard with us. Our queen would destroy her on sight."

Mathadar fluttered his wings in frustration. "We will visit this young queen and if she commands us to intervene on her behalf, we will do so."

"But what will we do with her after that, Commander?" The males around him all began talking over each other, each with an opinion about how to proceed. "We must not allow a young queen to perish."

Bringing up one hand to silence them, their commander stated sternly, "Let us solve one problem at a time this day. We waste precious time she does not have debating the obvious."

Pharon spread his wings. "We'll fly. It's faster." Jumping into the air, he took flight as the others followed suit.

Mathadar's mind filled with images of a young defense-less queen being harmed. The thought of his people turning over one of their own to be slaved out lit his anger on fire. He flapped his wings with a vengeance, racing to get to her in time. Within moments they landed near a platform.

Rather than a Draconian queen, there was a strange alien queen. He didn't think he'd ever seen someone of her species before. His translator was loaded with hundreds of languages. After racking his brain, he couldn't ever remember speaking to a being such as her on any planet he'd ever visited.

The auctioneer appeared to be a local citizen, a Balarian. He casually ripped the front of her fragile clothing away to reveal the swell of her creamy breasts. Each was decorated with a delicate pink tip. Draconian queens didn't have large breasts because they didn't nurse young. Some species did and he'd always been fascinated by them.

Mathadar's mouth went dry watching her struggle against the ropes wrapped around her tiny wrists. Her fleshy mounds bounced in the sunlight. An image of her moving naked on top him popped into his brain just like that. White-hot anger spiked through this mind that he would create perverted images in this situation. Such thoughts proved he was no decent male.

He watched them hoist her arms above her head, leaving her feet dangling off the platform. Though she tried with all her might, the diminutive queen couldn't get enough purchase to kick them off her. The male handler just laughed and smacked at one of her exposed breasts. Mathadar's cock jerked when he saw a handprint appear on her pale skin. Something was definitely wrong with this brain today. Never before had Mathadar been as ashamed of this own thoughts and responses as he was this day.

Something about seeing the slaver run his hand over her stomach brought every protective instinct to the fore. When the male's hand began to slip down the front of the thin cloth covering her queenly treasures, Mathadar surged forward. "Stop. I demand to know what you have done with the young Draconian queen."

The Balarian turned to face him, as did most of the other beings in the crowd. "She was purchased a few moments ago. Our current offering is much more exotic." Glancing between the interloper and the woman for sale, he asked curiously. "Do your queens allow you to own play-things?" Grabbing a handful of the long filaments growing out of the queen's head, he brought them to his nose. "She smells like flowers. Her body is strong and resilient. Such a female would stand up to hard use by a group of Dragon warriors. Would you care to start the bidding?"

Before Mathadar could respond, words flew fast and furious from the alien queen's lips. "I command you to kill my abductors and free me immediately." Shocked that her language was already loaded in his translator, his eyes found hers. The emotion in her eyes hooked him in. Her words spoke directly to his heart and soul. When she spoke again her voice was tinged with desperation and fake bravado. "Draconian warriors are obligated to follow orders given by a queen. I'm more queenly than any woman you're ever gonna meet. Now get me the hell outta here."

Her words lit a fire underneath him. Without hesitating, he pulled out his laser pistol and unloaded it into the male attempting to auction her off. Grabbing the side of the platform, Mathadar jumped up and kicked the dead body down to the ground. He was vaguely aware that the entire city square had erupted into total chaos. His second team of warriors converged on the scene and his crew began to disperse the group. Since the locals were not letting their hostages go without a fierce fight, his warriors were forced to kill several more of her captors in the process.

Willing his eyes to remain on her face, Mathadar tucked his wings respectfully behind him. Dropping to one knee, he pressed one palm to the ground in the traditional pose of respect and submission to a queen.

"Hey big guy, I'm up here." Her voice sounded off over the sound of laser fire.

Rising to his feet, he asked sincerely, "Are you well, my queen?"

Shooting him an exasperated look, his new queen began

pulling on her bonds again. "Hell no, I'm not well. In case you haven't noticed, I'm still tied up and half naked. Untie me, now."

Flipping open a burning implement, it sliced through the thick rope with very little effort. Pulling her hands down, she ran the fingers of one hand over one wrist the way people are wont to do when they're injured. She seemed small and delicate to his eyes, with no claws or hard plating to protect her tender bits. Catching his eye, she nodded. "Now get me the hell outta here."

"Where do you wish to go, my queen?"

"We need to discover where they've taken Teladora. She's the Draconian girl you were asking about."

"Warriors may not pursue queens, particularly young queens. It is considered a crime among my people."

"She's in danger." Frowning at him, she growled, "Look, forget it. You're not pursuing the young queen, I am. You're simply following my commands. Does that work for you?"

Being spoken to directly by the lovely creature almost stole Mathadar's ability to speak, but asking his approval was downright confusing. Perhaps it was a test of some sort. Instead of responding verbally, he simply nodded his understanding. Awestruck—that's what his father would call his current state—awestruck and worried.

This new alien queen was all business. "Good. She was bought by some huge, wiry reptilian guy. He looked all kinds of angry when he dragged her outta here. We need to find her, now."

He found his voice. "It will be as you say, my queen," he mumbled.

Wrapping his hands around her waist, he lifted her and jumped from the platform down to the pavement before gently releasing her the moment her feet touched the ground. Stalking over to a small group of his men, they began speaking using the fast and loose jargon warriors resort to when time is of the essence. "Our new queen is targeting the young one. Need to scout for reptilian ships. Fallen queen must be secured immediately."

"We're on it," Pharon abruptly responded. "Scouts, take to the air with me."

Several groupings of two and three warriors took to the sky, while the others regrouped to plan strategy. The city square was a virtual ghost town at this point with bodies strewn about.

Mathadar began devising a plan in his mind to track down and rescue the younger queen. He couldn't allow harm to come to either of them. "We need to secure the alien queen away from the city. Dar, Ralen, and Sparn will take her to shuttle one and remain locked down on the tarmac until we secure the youngling."

A soft, feminine voice sounded off behind them. "That's a no-go. I'm going with you to rescue my friend."

Turning to face their demanding new queen, Commander Mathadar advised against her current course of action. "Reptilians are a ruthless breed. Their humanoid biology is mixed with that of lower lifeforms. Unlike dragon warriors, they lack self-control. Our prior interactions have turned into a fighting frenzy. Draconian queens are built for fighting. You are small, frail, and no match for a reptilian warrior. Allow us to fight this battle alone, my queen. We have taken note of your commands and will not fail you."

She took a step closer to him, teeth denting her bottom lip. If the pensive look on her pretty face was any indication, she was trying to figure out if his word could be trusted. Apparently today that was not to be because after careful consideration, she shook her head. "I'm sorry, but I don't know you. I'm willing to risk everything—including my life—to save my new friend, but I won't leave her fate to a bunch of men I don't even know."

Mathadar had no choice but to follow her orders. The scouts touched down and Pharon was at his side whispering in his ear within a micron. "We found only one reptilian vessel. It is nestled in an isolated area less than an arc from our current location." Glancing between him and their new queen, he asked incredulously, "We aren't taking her into battle, are we?"

Shooting his friend an exasperated look, Mathadar whispered, "She refuses to be left behind."

"She won't survive a battle against reptilians."

The commander ignored his medic's prolific warning. "New plan. Surround our new queen. We make for the reptilian shuttle. It's within a short jump of our current location."

"Give me a weapon. I can fight."

Cursing under his breath, Mathadar pulled a spare laser pistol from his belt and handed it over to her.

Pulling off his personal shield, he attached it to her ripped shirt to hold the two pieces of cloth together over her exposed breasts. Her eyes softened slightly, making him think covering her exposed flesh had been the right choice. Why he'd done that he didn't know. It just seemed like the right decision. Jerking his head slightly to the left, he tried to get his thinking back on track. He was used to following the commands of a queen, just not one who appeared so small and fragile.

This small queen with the pretty eyes made him feel things. She roused inappropriate images of breeding in his mind. Those were dangerous thoughts for a non-breeder to have floating around in his head.

Wrapping one arm around her, Mathadar turned to lead the way, trying his best to focus on the coming battle. Once they were in the air, she seemed light as a blade of grass. Something about having her soft, warm body against his felt more right than anything he'd ever known. Their flight was far too short in duration for his liking.

Alighting at the edge of forested area, he concealed them behind a large rock outcropping. His arm came out protectively in front of her as his keen senses picked up sounds of the enemy. She edged closer to him, pressing her soft body to his side. Thinking even for a moment that she liked to be close to him as much as he liked having her near was sheer foolishness.

Still, when her hand came out to rest on his arm he instinctively flexed his muscle. It was intended to be a gentle reminder of his strength. Her eyes flew up to his. There was less worry and more trust, likely because they'd flown together. Had the small wingless queen enjoyed being carried through the air in his arms? She must have because her hands gripped him tighter as though she were laying claim to him somehow.

Then it happened. She made the mating gesture. Looking down at her perfectly straight, albeit strangely blunted teeth, he knew it wasn't the proper time or place for such pursuits. Yet he couldn't resist returning the gesture, showing off all his razor-sharp teeth. Her mouth dropped open, apparently awestruck by the brazen display of his very best feature.

Knowing she selected him from all the others as her protector both thrilled and worried him. Some small part of him wanted to wrap her up in his arms and never let her go. It was an ill-advised thought to have running around in his head when danger was near.

4 WOMANLY WILES

CASSANDRA

Something about smiling at the bulky warrior lit a fire behind his eyes. She worried that he was so used to being dealt pain and misery from his queen that he'd been easily dazzled by a simple smile. It hurt her heart to think he could value something so elementary.

She'd been a little shocked when he returned the gesture. A full-on smile looked weird on him because of the two rows of razor-sharp teeth. Honestly, he looked like he could literally bite her head off with very little effort. Things were moving so fast that Cassandra decided to file that away as a problem for another day. Right now the priority was rescuing Teladora.

Crouching down behind a nearby boulder, they watched the reptilians preparing their ship for departure. Their stark appearance and stern manner was off-putting to say the least. They were smaller than Draconian warriors and moved stiffly like they wanted to drop down onto all fours to move more freely. Their forked tongues slithered out to test the air several times. Instead of wearing shoes they had sharp claws, which tore at the ground when they walked, kicking up dust with every step. Everything about the creatures was unnerving.

Cassandra noticed that they'd bought several slaves. In addition to Tela, they had an assortment of other living beings. The slaves were all different sizes, and some even had fur covering their bodies. Even though a few appeared more animal than human, the look in their eyes told her they were sentient beings, fearful of what the future held in store for them. It was personally humiliating to admit to herself that she couldn't easily separate the people from the animals in her own mind. Did that make her a bad person? The voice that whispered through her mind said yes. It made her feel foolish and backward. On this strange, colorful planet up was down and down was up.

The commander waited patiently for his warriors to surround the encampment. He used subtle noises and hand gestures to communicate, clearly coordinating a plan of attack. The Draconian warriors fell into an easy interaction, leading her believe this wasn't their first sneak attack. That should make her really uncomfortable, but instead it made her feel more secure. These brutal warriors clearly knew what they were doing and they were on her side. This turn of fortune was more than she could have hoped for, and she meant to make the best of it.

For some reason the reptilians had elected to land in a remote area on the outskirts of the city rather than on one of the two designated landing pads.

Their odd choice made more sense when several members of their crew came out of the thicket carrying crates. It became immediately apparent that they were scavenging resources from the planet.

Clinging onto the nice commander who rescued her like a damsel in distress was embarrassing. However, he was her rock at the moment. His protectiveness was just the balm she needed to soothe her battered soul. He'd been a good sport about her sticking close.

His stern voice turned gentle when he looked over his shoulder to catch her eye. "Remain under cover until we dispatch the enemy. We cannot concentrate on the fight if our attention is divided by protecting you." The commander's hastily whispered directions made sense.

"It will be as you say, Commander."

His head whipped around in her direction and his horns fell back slightly. His reaction coupled with the fact that his mouth was hanging open led Cassandra to believe that perhaps parroting his own responses back to him had been shocking. He recovered quickly, his hands drawing both weapons from his hip holsters.

The moment before he turned from her was wrought with tension and something akin to admiration. The huge dragon warrior had muscles on top of muscles. His blue skin had a scale pattern that ran underneath no small amount of scarring. His stark deep blue eyes searched hers for a brief moment as his chest rose and fell.

This man was putting his life in danger for no other reason than she'd asked it of him. The reality of their situation slammed through her mind, almost taking her breath away. Reaching out one hand toward him, she murmured, "Thank you for helping us. I appreciate it more than you will ever know."

An almost imperceptible shake of his head communicated his bewilderment. "Warriors fight on behalf of our queens. It's what we do."

Bringing her hand to her mouth, tears welled up in her eyes. "Please be careful," she murmured.

Why she was so emotional about this man was a

complete mystery. He was a virtual stranger. Why did she care so much after knowing him for only moments? Maybe this is what going crazy felt like.

Turning without another word, he made a high-pitched sound, which must have been the signal for the others to engage. All the warriors engaged the enemy at the same time, each targeting a different reptilian.

From her vantage point, Cassandra had to admit that it wasn't much of a fight. The Draconian warriors were quick, lethal, and didn't hesitate when it came time to kill. The moment the last reptilian fell, she surged forward from her position, intending to board the vessel. Her feet hit the ground hard as she ran for the ship.

Unfortunately, she only got a few feet before the unthinkable happened. One of the enemies stepped out of the bush in front of her. With a quick glance down, she caught sight of a weapon in his hand. It was pointed directly at her stomach. Being all too aware of how awful it was to linger near death with a laser burn through the gut, she stopped in her tracks.

His expression was arrogant. He was very pleased with himself—and why shouldn't have been? He managed to escape being killed by the Draconian warriors and recaptured his hostage.

"I knew they would come for their young queen. The Draconians are so predictable."

The man's voice was sinister, arrogant, and self-assured. Though she had a weapon in her hand, he didn't fear her. When he pulled the trigger, she waited for her life to flash before her eyes. Instead, something strange happened. The moment the laser got close to her body, an energy field activated, deflecting most of the beam and absorbing the rest.

She'd forgotten about the shield the commander

attached to her clothing. In the space of a heartbeat, the tables turned. Quickly raising her own weapon, Cassandra fired straight toward his face. As luck would have it, he didn't have a shield.

The look of pure mortification on his face right before his head disappeared gave her pause. His body fell with a thud, first to his knees, then onto the ground. Thick brown body fluids gushed from the opening where his head used to be, wetting the ground.

Cassandra looked down at the gun in her trembling hand. She'd never killed another person in her entire life. Granted, she'd wanted to a bunch of times but never had the opportunity to test her willpower in that regard. An image of Tela's youthful face popped into her mind as she grasped the weapon tightly in her hand. She had to save the innocent young girl. Nothing else mattered. Making a run for the door of the ship, she realized most of the warriors were already on board, clearing a path.

Shoving her way past them, she stumbled onto something. It was the commander's body. Casting the weapon aside, she tore at the front of his uniform. It was wet with his blood. Trying to press down on the wound, she shouted for a medic. Everything seemed to be happening in slow motion. The battle heated up again when several reptilians rushed into the dimly lit corridor. The flash of their weapons, the smell of burned flesh, and the growing pool of blue blood spreading out underneath the commander had her screaming for help again.

One of his men shoved her out of the way, dropping to his knees to place the dying man in stasis. She recognized the procedure, as it had been used on her multiple times over the years. Stasis would preserve his bodily functions exactly as they were now so a fully trained trauma team could work on him back aboard their vessel.

Staring down at the blood on her hands, Cassandra tried to remember why she was there. Tela's face rose in her mind's eyes and she quickly staggered to her feet. Cassandra shoved aside that fact that their commander was down and she would be dead at this point if he hadn't given her his shield. The need to find Tela before something terrible happened to her became Cassie's all-consuming quest.

A scream rent the air, catching the notice of several of the Draconian warriors. They rushed in the direction of the sound and she followed at breakneck speed. Her feet pounded on the metal floor and another scream filled her ears as she pumped her arms to put on a burst of speed.

They burst into a dimly lit room to find the teen's arms tied above her head in the center of the room. The back of her clothing had been ripped open to reveal a trail of open wounds on her back. All hell broke loose as the warriors began hand-to-hand combat with the group of reptilians enjoying the young girl's scourging.

Cassie made her way to the center of the room, firing at a couple of males along the way. The moment she was at Tela's side she began working at the restraints holding her wrists. The young teen flipped around, her eyes a mixture of hurt and fury. "You came for me?"

"Of course I came for you. We discussed that, remember?"

She choked back a sob. "I can't believe you actually came."

Finally her hands came free and Tela collapsed onto the ground, with Cassie kneeling protectively at her side trying to pull up the uniform that was slipping down her shoulders. The room grew quiet around them. When the older woman looked around, she saw the battle was over. The warriors were gaping at them, clearly unsure how to proceed.

Cassie's voice crackled with emotion. "Get the hell out, all of you." Swallowing thickly, she added, "Bring us a medic, clear this ship of the reptilians, and lift off. Put as much distance between us and your Draconian vessel as possible."

There was a moment of shock, then the males scrambled to execute her commands, and in doing so gave them a moment to themselves. Cassie felt numb. After almost getting killed, the one warrior she'd connected with falling under enemy fire because she wore his shield, and then discovering the young teen had been abused, it was almost too much.

Nothing was going as she hoped today. The only silver lining was they were both still alive and for the moment free. If being a slave for years had taught her one thing it was that staying alive was no small feat.

Grasping onto her arms, Tela looked up at her. "How did you get here so quickly?" The hurt in her eyes was now mixed with curiosity.

Clearing her throat, Cassie forced some levity into her voice. "I used my feminine wiles on the warriors and they couldn't resist me. I charmed them right into doing our bidding."

Tela's face relaxed slightly. "You commanded and they obeyed."

"You're not wrong about that, my friend." A soft guttural sound from the doorway captured her attention. "I believe this is the medic. Will you allow him to look at your back?"

"It hurt my pride more than my body. A medical laser will have my wounds healed quickly."

Cassie eased her down to a sitting position and motioned the medic over. "Come. What's your name?"

"Pharon, my queen."

"My name is Cassandra. See what you can do about the wounds on her back."

"Yes, my queen. Will the two of you fight for the right to this vessel when she is healed?" His hands moved to his utility belt and he grabbed a medical device. He began running the laser healer deftly over her skin.

"Hell no. What's wrong with you that tearing each other apart is your first concern as soon as you patch someone up?"

"Among our people queens settle disputes by challenging each other in battle," Tela quickly explained. "I have no wish to challenge you, for I know you are not my enemy. My wish is to find my training ship and challenge whichever queen has my males."

The medic's eyes flashed up to Teladora's for a brief moment. "That is inadvisable, young queen. You are not in prime condition to challenge a healthy queen."

"I have no wish for her to begin thinking of them as *her* males." Tela's pout was kind of cute, but the medic was right about her being in no condition to fight. She seemed kind of sickly before, but after being scourged, she had dark circles under her eyes and her hands were trembling.

Changing the subject, Cassandra remarked, "You were the one working on the commander. Do you think he will survive?"

Without looking up, he responded, "Commander Mathadar is seriously injured. I had him taken to the medical unit and placed into an automated healing platform. It will take some time for the scanners to complete their work."

"He was injured because ..."

"Everyone is well aware of why he was injured."

Cassie closed her eyes. "I should have stayed back at the shuttle like he asked, then he wouldn't have felt compelled to give me his shield."

Pharon's lack of a reply was evidence that he agreed with her assessment. A good man might die because she refused to follow directions from the person commanding the mission.

"He gave you his shield and then went into battle? If he is fortunate enough to survive, he will be hailed as a hero."

"To my mind, he's a hero regardless of whether or not he survives. He rescued us. We live only because he intervened. I owe him a life debt."

Tela's eyes grew big. "Queens do not owe warriors life debts. It is their duty to sacrifice themselves for us." As soon as the words came out of her mouth, the girl's eyes closed. "I'm sorry I said that. Males should be valued the same as a queen. I can see that now."

Cassandra laid a hand over Tela's. "I'm happy to know that you're coming to understand your own mind and making decisions for yourself about how you fit into the world around you. I'm proud to have you as a friend."

The medic looked from one to the other as he finished closing the wounds on her back. The silence spun out, with each of them thinking over the events of the day from their own perspectives.

5 HUNTED

MATHADAR

Drifting in and out of consciousness for he knew not how many cycles, the commander's sleep was filled with all sorts of fanciful dreams. He imagined a warm gentle female voice tenderly calling to him, whispering in his ear that he was needed and desired. Soft fingers caressed his skin, stirring his soul. Cool compresses moistened his scalp, teasing his horns. The flutter of warm hands drifting along his wings finally startled him awake.

Blinking up at the alien female he rescued brought it all back in a flash. She'd chosen him as her protector and perhaps the first of her breeders. There was no mistaking the mating gesture she made to him. She displayed her blunt white teeth for him to see and he'd reciprocated. Here she was making the gesture all over again. A surge of pride whipped through his body at being selected for breeding. Making young was every warrior's dream come true.

Memories of the battle came rushing to the fore. Gods of Chaos, the warriors brought her on board their ship. Struggling to sit up, he tried to call out to Pharon but only a horse whisper escaped his throat.

A hydration pouch appeared in front of his mouth and he took a long, greedy drink before speaking. "You are not safe aboard this ship, my queen."

Her hand drifted over to his shoulder. "They got rid of all the reptilians. I promise you're perfectly safe. You should lie back down and rest."

Pausing a moment to take in his surroundings, Mathadar realized they were still on the enemy vessel. Rubbing his forehead, he struggled to get his mind around what was going on. "I need Pharon."

His longtime friend's voice sounded off from nearby. "I am here, Commander."

Scooting to the edge of the healing platform, he looked around for the medic. "Bring me up to speed."

Pharon strolled over and began scanning him with a handheld unit. "We have been claimed by the human queen. She instructed us to commandeer the reptilian vessel and we are currently being pursued by our former queen."

"How long have I been down?"

"Five cycles, sir. You should not be on your feet yet. We had to fabricate lung and spleen tissue. Our new queen insisted that I keep you sedated until I was certain the grafts took. You need time to heal."

"Who's in command of this vessel?"

Laying the scanner aside, he explained, "Queen Cassandra has been making all the command decisions, with recommendations from the crew and the young queen we rescued. You were correct. The youngling is unascended."

Queen Cassandra's angry voice sounded off. "Don't talk about Tela that way. She's fine just the way she is."

Their new queen was protective of her younger counterpart, as a queen should be. To his mind this was proof that she was every inch a queen. "When is the challenge?"

Pharon caught his eye, holding his gaze. Much was communicated by the look. "There will be no challenge. The two females operate as a team, much like warriors. It is strange to see, but they seem to share a mother/daughter-type bond."

Holding his hand over his still-healing chest, Mathadar articulated their major concern. "We have an accompaniment of only thirty warriors. It isn't enough to care for one, much less two queens. We need to replenish our ranks if we are to have any chance of survival."

"You are correct. The twenty-eight warriors that survived the battle are barely enough to keep this ship functioning around the clock."

"We need a mother ship. Our only chance is to pick off one of the weaker queens and assume command of her ship."

Pharon handed him an electronic tablet. "That was our assessment as well. The crew worked up several options for you to review."

Their new queen spoke up. "I think we should keep this ship as well. I know it's smaller, but it is battleworthy and we'd have a better chance if we form a small armada."

"Your battle tactics make sense, my queen. However, we may not end up with enough warriors to safely crew two ships."

"Unless we manage to escape Exion space, Tela will one day want her own ship. We should bear that in mind when making plans for the future. Though she is intent on finding her old training ship and challenging the queen controlling it, she may have to settle for something less impressive."

"It will be as you wish, my queen," he responded curtly, biting his tongue.

Anger flashed in her pretty blue eyes. "Don't ever say those words to me again, Commander. I'm serious. If you have something further to say, give me the dignity of speaking it."

Straightening at the reprimand, he pulled himself together. "With respect my queen, I do not think you understand the gravity of our situation. You have a mere thirty warriors standing alone against an infinite number of motherships, each with a capable and experienced queen in command. Though they might be willing to let you slip their grasp as alien queens are little more than a nuisance, they will track us until the end of times to get the unascended queen back. They have an irrational hatred against the unascended and only allowed her to live knowing she would be tortured as recompense for their harshness with other beings in this sector. They will never allow her to go free."

Understanding dawned in her pale blue eyes. "Then we run. We'll get as far away from the other queens as possible."

"You would do well to abandon me on a nearby world and escape while they attempt to capture me." The teen stepped forward from the doorway with her wings drawn up high and tight behind her small body and her horns standing up bravely. Clearly the youngling was ready to sacrifice herself, but his new queen was having none of it.

Stepping forward, one hand came out to land on the younger female's shoulder. "I'm not abandoning you. We made a deal, remember?"

Nodding slightly, her horns relaxed. "We're a team. That was our agreement."

"This is a dangerous choice you make, my queen. Would you truly die in battle to protect a young queen who failed to ascend?" Pharon asked quietly.

Pivoting to face him, she blocked his view of Tela with her body. "Yes. Human women don't care about rites of ascension. Dying wouldn't be my first choice, but if it comes down to it, yes. Either we both escape this sector or we both go down fighting."

"Queens do not protect queens."

"I can't leave her to such a nasty fate. Don't you understand? She's young and needs our protection."

"I am not weak, human." Tela's disgruntled voice rang out behind her, yet no one acknowledged her statement.

"I do understand your need to protect the youngling, but you must understand something as well, my queen," Mathadar quietly explained. "The Draconian queens rule for as far as we can fly in any direction at maximum speed. We could fly for the duration of our lifespan and never break free of their space."

Folding her arms over her stomach, she refused to acknowledge the futility of running. "What you say can't be true." Gesturing to herself with one hand, she said, "I'm from the Naxis, not Exion. I was brought here against my will. If I can come here in a few years, then we can get back in a similar amount of time."

"I wish that were the case. Do you know your way back to your human home world? Can you show us the way?"

Shaking her head, the deliciously stubborn queen seemed about to break.

"You commanded me to kill the only beings who knew the way back to your sector of space. If not for that, I might have been able to track them down and force them to lead us back there."

Liquid began to slowly leak from her eyes, drizzling a thin trail down her delicate skin. Growing more alarmed by the moment, Mathadar began to panic. "Pharon, something is very wrong. Our new queen is leaking. Make it stop."

"Calm yourself, Commander," his friend responded lightly. "This has happened several times over the last few cycles. Human queens are different from the queens we have known. Salty water leaks from their eyes when they are overwhelmed, sad, or extremely happy. This emotional overflow is as normal for them as the anger displayed by our own queens when they are experiencing heightened emotions."

Sliding off the healing platform, he reached for her. Mathadar was surprised when she moved closer to him. He drew her into the circle of his arms and tucked her head under his chin. Why he did that, he didn't know. Perhaps because it was a protective pose and she seemed in need of his support.

Pharon stood gaping at him before turning on his heel and stalking out of the room.

His new queen cuddled closer to him. "I messed this up in every conceivable way, didn't I?" she asked.

"All will be well, my queen. Though we are but simple warriors, we will devise an effective strategy, even if it means taking out one mothership at a time for the duration of our lifetime."

"I'm really sorry."

Her apology confused him. Queens didn't apologize to warriors. It simply wasn't done. Mathadar didn't know where his head was on this subject. Queens laid claim to another's warriors from time to time. Unless they were high-status breeders, no one seemed to care much. He was convinced that some queens thought it an amusing game of skill to steal warriors. This was the first time he ever felt a queen valued him in the least.

The delicate human queen needed him and he had to find a way to keep her safe. All other considerations were secondary at this point. Having her so close and vulnerable had him doing things he'd normally never consider doing with a queen. He'd never wrapped his arms around a queen or soothed one when she was emotional. It felt good to be valued in this way.

He found himself wrapping the long strands growing from her head around his fist. Tugging it gently back, he forced her look into his eyes. "From this moment forward, you will allow me to make the decisions I see fit to keep you safe."

They were so close that they were breathing the same air. A bond was forming between them, the type of bond that normally only formed between breeders with their queen. Pure male pride surged through his chest when she lowered her eyes and acquiesced to his demand. "I'll do as you say when it comes to safety, I promise."

"Do you tell the truth? You will follow my lead?"

Her eyes became softer and her voice trembled when she spoke. "I will follow your lead. You got hurt protecting me. I was foolish to insist upon coming with you. I won't put you in danger again." Her pink tongue came out to lick her bottom lip and her front teeth dented a crease along it.

He watched her face with the kind of fascination born of a lifetime of unfulfilled need. "Everything about you is designed to lure a warrior in, make him do your bidding. Normally obedience is given because failing to do so results in a warrior being terminated. I do not know how I feel about willingly serving a queen simply because she bewitches me."

Running her hand over his bulging bicep, she sighed. "Human women don't like to have their males fearful of displeasing them. We value cooperation and watch out for our males. We never leave a man behind."

"How many, my queen?"

Her delicate brow creased. "How many what?"

"How many males will you take to your side? I find myself reluctant to share certain things with other males. I think perhaps this makes me a poor choice in breeding partners for a lovely queen like yourself."

She seemed pensive but didn't respond to his query. Then again, he hadn't thought she would.

6 POKER FACE

CASSANDRA

Commander Mathadar spent the better part of each day on the bridge engaged in the serious business of playing cat and mouse with his former queen. She'd followed them and seemed intent on capturing and punishing them for their defection. She'd gotten very little face-to-face time with him lately.

A fist came flying at her face so fast that Cassie barely ducked in time to miss it.

Tela's smug voice sounded off. "You are slow and easily distracted today, humon."

"Aren't you a barrel of laughs."

Tela reveled in mispronouncing "human." If she were human, she would definitely be considered a prankster.

Cassandra was still trying to figure out an amusing way to mispronounce "Draconian," but nothing was coming quickly to mind. She marveled at how happy and carefree Tela was. The young girl was as playful as Cassie could ever remember a teen being. She had a delightfully mischievous personality and was always up for a laugh.

"You worry too much about your commander. He will come if you send for him."

Throwing another misguided punch, Cassie stepped back to avoid the counter punch. "I want him to choose to spend time with me, not come because he's summoned."

Snorting a laugh, Tela plopped down on the floor of the training room. "I don't know how humans ever get around to breeding. Among my people the queen summons her choice in males and he is more than happy to accommodate her request for mating. You are making easy things hard."

Sitting down to face her friend, Cassie teased, "It sounds like you have a crush on a male from your training ship."

"I selected three breeders, but one is extraordinary."

Scooting closer, Cassie wrapped her arms around her knees. "Do tell. What's he like?"

"Trace is the most attractive male I've ever seen. He's nice and well trained to attend to the needs of a queen."

Motioning with one hand, Cassie encouraged the girl to tell all. "Come on, dish all the details."

"He doesn't have the bulk of a warrior, but his muscles are taut and well developed. He's punctual and when he gives me a body massage, my queenly parts notice, not that he ever touches me there. I prefer him sleeping beside me to all the other males who were sent for my perusal."

"How about his personality?"

"He notices everything that goes on aboard the ship and tells me all the details. Nothing happened on my mother's ship that I didn't know about. Sometimes we stayed up all night talking and drinking refreshing beverages."

"You really miss him, don't you?"

Tela's wings jerked in an aggressive movement and her anger flared. "He's *meant* to be mine. I can't stand the thought of another queen touching him. She can have all the others, just not Trace."

Before Cassie could respond, klaxons began sounding. They both jumped to their feet and headed for the bridge. The males standing guard outside the training room door kept pace with them.

Sliding onto the bridge, Cassie saw the face of an older queen filling the view screen. She was shouting commands at Mathadar. His totally blank expression spoke volumes about how little he was enjoying the interaction.

"Mathadar, I'll take great pleasure in removing your entrails myself if you don't follow my orders. Turn your ship around and rendezvous with me immediately."

Cassandra strolled forward to stand by the captain's chair. Placing a hand on his shoulder, she stared into the Draconian queen's shocked eyes. "He won't be doing any of that and if you dare to come within a hundred parsecs of this ship, I'll make you regret the day you were born. Now, back off."

The older queen's eyes flew from the woman tossing threats her way to the commander. "You dare to replace me with a weak alien queen? You will regret the day you turned your back on me!"

"Again, you're talking to the wrong person. I'm in charge of this ship, so how's about you direct a little of that vitriol my way?"

"You are ridiculously brazen when you are parsecs beyond my reach." Her slightly luminescent eyes and the soft sheen of sweat coating her skin gave the brawny queen a truly unappealing quality. "Know this: I will not allow you to steal away my warriors, nor will I permit you to shelter the failed queen."

"Strange that you're still tossing around orders like

anyone here cares what you have to say. I've heard you worship Tarken in place of the goddess these days. You should take a break from commanding your own vessel and get some help."

"You are not worthy to speak my name."

"That would be tough since none of your warriors ever mentioned your name. They call you 'former queen.' It's almost like they don't respect you at all."

"Why are you baiting me? You must know that I can rip you limb from limb."

Taking a step forward, Cassandra knew it would make her appear larger and more dominant in the view screen. It was something a small being needed to compete on an equal footing in this situation. "I'll tell you what I know. If we get half a chance, I'm going to board your vessel, kick your ass, and rip that nice ship right out from under you." Folding her arms over her chest and sounding a thousand times more certain than she felt, Cassandra conjured the most menacing tone she could manage. "That's how it's done around these parts, right? Queens challenge each other and winner takes all. I might be smaller, but I'm faster, smarter, and more resourceful in a battle than you were on your best day."

"You're being absurd."

"Am I? You've never challenged a human before. For all you know we might shift into vicious animals or have the ability to disappear at will. The 'verse is infinite and you've only challenged beings from one small quadrant."

The woman pulled her head up, clearly taken aback. "I don't believe you can do any of that."

"Don't worry yourself about my abilities. Think about all the ways someone like you can die. When I catch up with you, if you're really nice, I'll let you pick the manner of your own death. That's the only quarter I'll ever give you."

Jerking her chin toward the warrior at the communications relay, Cassandra gestured for them to cut the feed.

The moment the screen went blank, Tela spoke up. "She's right. You can't do any of that. I've sparred with you and we both know you'd never survive a challenge from me, much less her."

Rolling her eyes, Cassandra deadpanned back, "Yeah, but *she* doesn't know that."

Mathadar spoke without looking at her. "What did you hope to accomplish by infuriating our former queen? Even though she is still many solars from reaching us, she will take her retribution upon you in the most painful way possible, my queen."

"On earth humans have a game we take very seriously. It's called poker. I grew up playing this game of strategy with my father. Rule number one is to never allow your opponent to figure out what you've got up your sleeve. In this case, your former queen has no idea what I'm capable of, how many weapons we have, or which of us is even doing the pursuing at this point."

Turning his head to gape at her, he responded, "I am fairly certain she is pursuing us."

Shooing Mathadar a hot look, Cassie shook her head. "Not any longer. Allowing her to chase us over large distances makes us prey in her eyes. She thought all this time that she was in control. Now she's doubting herself."

"You honestly mean to challenge her, do you not?" Mathadar's whispered words were choked with emotion.

Moving closer to him, she responded sagely, "The only way out of this situation for us is through her. You know what I'm saying is true."

"There are older and weaker queens in the area. We could successfully target one of them."

"No. If we do that then we run the risk of her interfering with the battle. We might be able to win against one ship, but not two. Unless I miss my guess, the other queens are either unaware of our situation or are happy to let your former queen deal with us. You said it yourself once. There's no glory in winning against a weak opponent."

"If you best an experienced queen, they won't see you as weak anymore."

"Right now we really don't have anything they want. There are just two disgraced queens and a handful of low-status warriors. Hell, they certainly don't value alien tech. This ship wouldn't be worth the effort of a quick battle to win it."

It was Pharon who pointed out the obvious. "When we take our former ship, it will be a worthy prize. It's a newer ship and reasonably well maintained. They'll be willing to fight to take it from you."

"Correct me if I'm wrong, but motherships are warships, right?"

"Yes!" Tela answered enthusiastically. "Once we have a warship under our feet with a full crew complement, we can fight on an equal footing."

"My best guess is if we win, the other queens will swarm us. We need to figure a way out of this sector before that happens."

"If we cannot escape the Exion, they will eventually bring us to heel."

"The only chance we've got is to take her mothership and immediately attack the nearest ship, increasing our firepower and resources. We need to think outside the box and do the last thing they expect every step of the way. Keep them off-balance and unsure what to expect."

Mathadar stood and closed the distance between them in a few steps. "I like this strategy. I too believe we should strike first and when they least expect it. Our queens tend to prefer to resolve their disputes with a physical challenge. They are larger and stronger than the females of other species, which gives them the advantage."

"I'm not trying to get myself killed or all of you captured, so we're going to have to work something else out there."

"I can't imagine what."

Turning to look at Tela, a sly smile crept onto Cassie's face. "That's good news. You received the same training as our new adversary. If you're having a hard time imagining possible alternative assaults, that means she's likely having the same problem."

"What are you thinking?"

"I'm thinking that she didn't get her supply of Tarken. She's clearly anxious, angry, and sweating up a storm. No one can think clearly under those circumstances. I say our first course of action is to send scouts to any planet nearby where she could secure more of the drug and buy it up. We'll trade whatever happens to be in the cargo hold. If she knows we have it, she'll be eager to continue tracking us. We can use that to our advantage."

Mathadar reached out to wrap one hand around each of her arms. "We can use this ship to set a trap and sneak aboard her vessel using the shuttles we kept. It would be easy to change up the transponder frequencies to match shuttles she still has in operation. I have contacts aboard her vessel, males I trust who might assist us."

"We'll still need a plan to take her down."

Tela stepped up. "I will join you in this battle. Perhaps one of us can distract her while the other engineers a solution that avoids bloodshed."

"On Earth we sometimes use tranquilizer darts to deliver a strong sedative. We could even put it in her food or send it into her sleeping quarters through an air vent. After she's incapacitated, we dump her on an isolated planet with a distress beacon and when another ship comes to pick her up, we repeat the same scenario."

"Queens do not fight this way. It is considered cowardly." The girl's disapproving tone of voice spoke volumes about her teachings on such techniques.

"Riddle me this, pumpkin. Why is it that the biggest, baddest bitches in the entire galaxy get to decide what kind of fighting is honorable? Does that sound very fair to you?"

Tela blinked once and then again as she thought over the question. "No, it does not seem very fair when you speak of it in that manner. It seems as though our queens are creating rules of warfare that ensure they will always be victorious."

"I agree. Therefore, we probably don't need to worry about fighting according to their rules. In fact, humans have a saying for situations like this: *All's fair in love and war.*"

When the expression on everyone's faces morphed into one of confusion, Cassandra clarified her train of thought. "It means playing by someone else's rules can put you at a disadvantage during a war and selecting a mate."

Pharon's bland question came almost immediately. "Does this mean you plan to take males against their wishes as well?"

"Do not question our queen in matters of mating, Pharon. You know it is not proper." Mathadar's warning was followed by him making eye contact with the other males, as if daring them to contradict him. He was sticking up for her in his own way.

Cassie stepped closer to the one man who always seemed to have her back. The more time she spent around him the surer she was that he might be her one. "It means that women are allowed to use any means necessary to win in battle or win a male's affections."

Mathadar almost smiled. "Some battles are more easily won than others, my queen."

His softly spoken words warmed her from the inside out. Stepping back, she snagged one of his hands in her own. Ignoring the other warriors who were looking everywhere except at her, she headed for the door. "We should create a strategic battleplan."

Tela walked over and dropped into the captain's seat, running her hands covetously over the armrests. "We'll be here when the two of you are finished with the ...mission planning."

7 HANDS ON A QUEEN

MATHADAR

He had no idea where his illustrious queen was leading him. Though she stated that she wished to engage in mission planning, it was clear this was not true. There was but one room aboard the vessel where all the systems necessary could be accessed and cross-referenced. It was the planning room, a private office off to the side of the bridge. They were going in the opposite direction. They would soon come upon the training rooms and after that the sleeping quarters allocated to those appointed to the command crew.

The guards assigned to watch over her would not leave even if ordered to do so. She had her hands on him, and that meant only one of two things among Draconians: She was either displeased and wished to scourge him, or their queen was a deviant and wished to be serviced by a plain warrior rather than a breeder.

The guards dropped back, whispering about their concerns.

"She means to breed him. I can see it in her eyes."

"That's perverse."

"Normally, I would agree."

When they rounded a corner, the guards' voices faded out. Within moments Mathadar could barely hear them again.

"Do you see any breeders aboard this vessel?"

"You're correct. When a queen's heat comes, she will choose the most worthy from whoever is available."

Though humans apparently did not possess the keen senses of the Draconians, Mathadar turned his head to pin them with a disapproving glare. That shut the babbling pair up and they broke apart to assume a more appropriate pose.

Cassandra's feminine voice drifted to his ears. "Are you all right, Commander?"

Swiveling his head around, Mathadar realized she came to stop in the corridor. He made a mistake in allowing the errant crewmembers to draw his attention away from their queen. "I am well, my queen." When she didn't respond immediately, he lowered his eyes submissively.

She tugged his hand, encouraging him to move closer. Mathadar stepped into her personal space without hesitation. Bringing her hand up underneath his chin, she tilted his head up to look into his eyes. "I want to spend some time talking about our mission and getting to know you better. Will you dine with me in my quarters, or do you want to go to the dining area?"

Mathadar froze, trying to understand her words. It was difficult to focus with her warm, soft hands on him. She wished to get to know him better, but in what capacity—as her commander or as a potential addition to her harem? Males did not have the right to choose, yet she was asking him to do so.

His head filled with a hundred questions. Was this a test? Did she think him simple? Was she trying to trap him into taking liberties in order to justify eliminating him? Mathadar realized he was allowing his anxieties to guide his mind into ludicrous places. Human queens were not like Draconian queens. Therefore, she might just be confused enough to believe that males should be given choices.

Her hand relaxed in his and she began to let go. He was taking too long to answer her. Panicking, he grasped her hand back and rushed to answer her question. "Queens lead and warriors follow. That is the natural order of our society. Still, since you ask my preferences, I will answer truthfully. Though I am but a simple warrior, I wish you to get to know me better as your commander and a potential male for your harem. It would be my honor to serve you until such time as true breeders can be secured for your pleasure."

Her mouth dropped open and she gaped at him. As the silence spun out between them, he began to worry that perhaps he had misspoken. Perhaps it was a test after all. If so, he failed miserably.

Finally, she laughed. "I'm not sure that I understand most of what you just said, but I got that you're okay with me getting to know you better. How's about we talk over dinner in the dining hall?"

Relief and excitement warred for the dominant position in his emotions. Apparently this little queen had an endless amount of patience for awkward warriors like himself. "I would be more comfortable dining in privacy, so all may not overhear our words." Being socially awkward in front of subordinates would not do, for they must see their commander as strong and capable.

As if she guessed his predicament, her eyes slid to the pair of guards standing twenty paces behind him. Her body straightened, she snapped a quick nod, and pulled her hand from his.

"Come, we will order food and discuss battle strategy."

When she turned to make her way to her quarters Mathadar followed, astonished that she put on her warrior's face. Her human face was expressive and he didn't know if he liked seeing it cleared of expression. It pained him somehow.

Then there was the loss of physical contact. It was more disappointing than he would have thought. His skin still tingled from the touch of her warm flesh against his. In his world queens didn't randomly touch warriors, unless he was unfortunate enough to provoke her ire. Their claws could wreak terrible damage on a male. By contrast, this human queen's hands were tipped with delicate claws that likely couldn't tear open fruit properly.

Among his kind physical strength ensured dominance. Draconian queens were larger than males and much more vicious in battle. For the first time in his life Mathadar could see that weakness as something other than a curse.

The moment they approached the door to her chambers, it slid open. Stepping over the threshold seemed somehow more meaningful with a human queen. Perhaps it was because he was at her side rather than several paces behind her as was required by a Draconian queen.

Mathadar cued the dining hall to send food on his portable com unit, asking for a selection of actual food rather than nutrition bars or the protein paste the males spread on doma bread.

Smiling at him, they sat on the only piece of furniture they could find aboard the reptilian vessel that was fit for a queen. "I hope you didn't order one of everything. A woman can only tolerate so much bland protein paste before she screams the walls down."

"I asked for high-quality foodstuffs, worthy of being consumed by a queen."

Leaning back, she draped one arm along the back of the settee. "I didn't know the paste came in different grades. After I was abducted by the Balarians, all I got to eat was some kind of watery soup. It had nuggets of whatever leftover vegetables they had on hand and was served cold. I know this probably sounds speciest, but it always smelled vaguely fishy."

Mathadar glanced away, his horns slipping back against his head. "It pains me that you were not fed properly while among the aquatics. I will pay close attention to ensure your food is of high quality while you are with us."

Her eyes dropped down to find the tip of his tail trailing across her delicate ankle. He pulled it back and hastened to draw her attention away from his indiscretion. "You were shocked to discover so much time had passed since you left Earth. Do you mind if I ask what you remember of your abduction and voyage to our sector of space?"

Her eyes rose and he tried not to notice how curious she was about his tail. She'd followed it with her eyes and leaned over slightly when he pulled it behind him.

Her sparkling blue eyes dimmed as she began speaking of her hardship. "I was separated from my group while hiking. I don't know of the exact manner in which they abducted me. I just remember waking up on their ship. At first they had me floating in a huge tube of pale blue liquid, with something soft plugging my nose and mouth. I was getting air, but it took me a few days to realize that whatever liquid they had me in was providing both hydration and nutrition. I assume it was just getting absorbed through my skin or something."

"What you are describing sounds like the containers

that are commonly used in this sector of space to transport live specimens."

"I think you're right about that. I could see other tubes with different kinds of strange animals. Now that I'm more familiar with the wide variation among different alien species, it seems likely they were people collected from other worlds. Most were sold off along the way, but a couple of them were rescued with me and are on board this vessel."

"They wish to stay with us and have been allocated crew positions. I did not think you would wish us to turn them away in their time of need. They have sharp minds and strong backs, much like Draconian warriors. I promise they will serve you well, my queen."

There was movement at the door and a warrior arrived with food stacked in metal containers. Mathadar came to his feet and extended a hand to his queen, who eagerly allowed him to assist her to a seat at the dining table. Though it was small, the table served its purpose.

"Everything looks amazing."

"I was told you declined our offer to prepare food for you several times. Is our food not to your liking?"

Twisting her small container slightly, she sighed. "I just didn't want to put the crew to any extra trouble. We're short-staffed as it is. They don't need to waste their time making gourmet meals for me."

"It is our pleasure to care for you to the best of our ability."

"We can worry about a more operational dining unit once we're fully crewed." Taking a bite, the look on her face morphed to one of bliss. "Now, where was I? Oh, we were talking about my trip here. At first they had me in the vat for what seemed like months. In retrospect, I now know it was more like years. I'm certain they sedated me, because I slept an awful lot. Humans only sleep six to eight hours per twenty-four-hour cycle, and I was out way more than that." Taking a sip of her hydration pouch, she continued, "I remember waking up and beating on the glass until my hands bled, turning the water purple. I guess my red blood mixing with the blue water explained the weird purple color."

Stopping to take another bite, she savored the flavors. Seeing a beautiful queen enjoy her food made Mathadar long to give her pleasure in other ways. Glancing away, he responded to her harrowing ordeal.

"The process for supporting fragile biological samples is very straightforward and regimented. The fluid must be cleansed every ten cycles and the biologic must be brought out of hibernation once every lunar cycle for at least fifty microns to keep the organs functioning properly."

Her eyes shot up at his. Her skin and lips paled as she nodded slightly. "That makes sense in relation to what I remember. Now that you mention it, the whole situation had a certain cycle feel to it. Anyway, for a long time I thought we were still on or near Earth, so I did everything I could to escape."

"From the clear tube?"

She nodded. "I eventually resorted to pulling the oxygen mask off my face," she explained quietly. "I figured they'd either remove me from the vat or I'd drown. Either way I'd be free."

Mathadar froze in place. He blinked once and then again before his voice returned. "It grieves me deeply to know you were so desperate that you were willing to sacrifice yourself to get free. It reminds me of animals who chew off their leg to get out of a trap."

Her eyes fell. "I just got to a point where I couldn't take

it anymore. Waking up in that cylinder over and over was more than I could bear. In any event, they put me in a cage. It was a pretty big one, but I had a hard time getting out of it. They were really angry with me. I think they really resented me for forcing them to take me out of their little lab."

"Did they strike you or assault you in ways not befitting a queen?"

She immediately understood his strange turn of a phrase. Mathadar didn't have the vocabulary to ask if she was forced to service the aquatic males. Relief surged through his chest when she gave a short shake of her head. Her human gestures were now familiar to him. He used them sometimes to aid in communication with her.

"No. I don't think we're biologically compatible. They treated me more like an annoying pet that had pissed on their floor. Before you ask, I never did that. They really disliked me and anything they discovered I disliked they increased and vice versa."

"They were not honorable males to torment a queen."

"They probably treat their own queens with respect. It's alien queens they have a problem with."

"A queen is a queen and it is not appropriate to make differences between them. Their treatment of you sealed their fate. Our crew left none standing."

"I honestly didn't think you'd get into a life-or-death brawl to save me."

"We are honorable and you are worth fighting for—and worth dying for."

"I'm really glad I met you, Commander."

8 DIFFICULT TO KILL

TELADORA

The moment the doors slid shut on the bridge, Tela spoke. "Seal off the bridge. I don't want any communications between this command crew and the others."

Reaching for the security console, one of the warriors spoke. "Our queen will not be pleased with this turn of events."

"Though I consider her a friend, I care not for the wishes of the human queen at this moment. I have communicated with the ship that was to be gifted to me and they are in route to our current location. Find the *Delacroy*, Navigator. Their transponder signal is one-five-five-hundred-ascend."

Tela was somewhat embarrassed that she'd chosen a transponder signal which stated her age, the number of males on her ship and the event that triggered her rise to power. It all seemed so pompous and glory-seeking to her quickly maturing mind. Now her only goal was to get back the life that was stolen.

"You mean to challenge the queen in control of that ship?"

Turning to look at the navigational officer, she shook her head slightly. "I would gladly do so to claim what is rightfully mine. However, that is unnecessary. I will soon be in control of my own ship. There was no other queen performing the rites of ascension at the same time as me. Therefore, there was no one to take my place aboard the *Delacroy*. They have reassigned my crew, including my breeders, to make supply runs between ships."

"That is a humiliation prime breeders should never be forced to endure."

"They punished them all for my failure to ascend."

"I have located their ship. If we plot a course to them at maximum speed, we will reach them before Queen Cassandra is finished breeding our commander."

"They are carrying munitions to resupply other ships in the fleet. It will take their chain of command at least a solar to discover they are missing. I want us together and enjoying the weapons upgrade they bring before that happens."

"Our rendezvous puts us at the intersection of three queen ships, and we still have our former queen in pursuit."

Gazing at their navigator, she asked, "What is your name, warrior?"

His eyes flew open and his wings startled. "My name is Direk, Queen Tela."

"Direk, I agree with Queen Cassandra on several issues. I tire of being prey, chased around by your former queen like a frightened forest creature. I wish to cover our exhaust trail and have an idea how to accomplish that with the supplies we have on hand."

"Queens lead and warriors follow."

"Say what is on your mind, Direk."

Glancing nervously around, his voice dropped a level.

"Do you not wish to work with the human queen to secure your vessel?"

"Of course not, for if I were to do such a thing my training ship would only be half mine. I mean to take my ship and join the human queen in battle, proving beyond a shadow of a doubt the worth of the unascended."

"It will be as you say, Queen Tela."

The warrior at the communications relay perked up. "I have established a link to the *Delacroy*, my queen."

"Put them on the main view screen."

The huge view screen lit up with the faces of multiple Draconian warriors. One stepped forward. "You yet live, my hatch mate."

Coming to her feet, Tela's wings fell open behind her and a smile spread across her face. "You will find that ascended or not, I am difficult to kill."

Several of her brothers all greeted her with smiles and glad hearts. "We were thrilled to receive your message, especially after being told that you were sold and would never return to Draconian society again."

"Yet here I am, about to take control of my training vessel after all."

"About that... I fear we will not last long as renegades."

"Though we have little chance of success, I am willing to fight for what is mine. Ours. Will you fight by my side, brothers?"

"Males do not have the right of choice, you know this, Teladora, Queen of the *Delacroy*. Do you actually test the loyalty and decency of your own hatch mates? Is this what our lives have come to?"

Taking a step closer to the view screen, Tela spoke to the heart of their problem. "I dare speak to our true issue, for it is too fantastical to credit as being truthful. In case we do not meet and I do not take command of the *Delacroy*, there is something you all must know."

"What is it? Are you well?"

"I am well, but I daresay every other queen in the fleet is infected."

"There is a plague amongst the queens? We must alert the healing center on Dracon immediately."

"No. I command silence on the coms. Let me get this out while I still have the stomach to tell my story."

"Speak, sister queen. I would know who to kill for harming you this day."

"It is nothing like that. It's to do with the cave of ascension." Taking a deep breath, she began her story. "When I entered the cave of ascension and walked through the pool, I saw why the waters were glowing. Millions of tiny luminescent larvae swam in the waters. When my head went below the waterline they began clawing with their tiny tentacles to get inside my body. They forced themselves into my nose, eyes, and other orifices."

Her brothers' expressions turned horrified. "Gods of Chaos, they attempted to invade your body and take root?"

"Yes. When I crawled from the waters, I began to cough. They left behind something slimy everywhere they touched. It tasted and smelled so putrid that I threw up and my body released feces. Everything that came out was riddled with the tiny luminescent larvae. I could see many dead and others writhing in my vomit. Seeing such a sight made me become sick all over again. I threw up until my throat burned like fire."

Her brothers looked at each other in astonishment. After a short silence one spoke. It was Calek, the youngest. "I don't understand. Why would the queens insist upon a rite for their precious daughters that gave them parasites?"

"I do not know but suspect the truth is very simple. Daughters are no more precious to them than sons. It seems all to do with the parasites. The other queens were horrified that I had killed so many of the larvae. They picked through my leavings, rescuing as many of the tiny creatures as possible, rushing them back to the water, even as I lay sick and heaving on the ground. Our mother was there. She acted like the larvae were her young and I was a mere host."

Wrapping her arms around her waist, she waited for her brothers to process the magnitude of what she was telling them. Images of her furious mother rose in her mind:

After carrying the tiny larvae back to the pool with several other women, she stood staring down at her daughter with an expression of revulsion stamped onto her face. "You are too weak to ascend and therefore mean nothing to me now." Grabbing her up by the throat, she flung Teladora toward the other queens. Turning her back, she walked from the cave without looking back.

Struggling to get ahold of her emotions, she stated, "It was more horrible than I even have words to say."

Instead of her brothers speaking up it was Direk, their navigator. "You suspect all the queens are infected since they must successfully complete the rite to ascend."

Tela nodded. "It stands to reason that if the larvae are parasites that can take control of the queen they inhabit, all our females are the hosts."

Calek's eyes grew wild, his voice panicked. "Are you saying our entire society is ruled by these parasites?"

Pain shot through her chest and her heart knew the answer, but it was still difficult to accept. Throwing up her hands, Tela began to pace. "I do not know, brother. All I know is what I saw with my own eyes."

"If this is true, it would explain their hatred of the unascended. They see you as murderers of their young."

"This explains many things about our culture," Direk said. "Think about it for a moment. The queens control their numbers, while they breed males prolifically. We are highly expendable, born only to serve. In all the 'verse no females are as cold to their males as our queens are to us. They are even horrible to their breeders."

Warmth blossomed in her chest, chasing away the cold. "Speaking of breeders, where are mine?"

"They are here and safe, sister queen. You know we would look out for them as you asked."

Feeling excitement spread through her body, Tela choked out, "I wish to speak to Trace."

Her brother's hand moved to the com station and suddenly the image blinked to a busy dining area. She could see warriors moving around, efficiently taking trays of food and moving to sit at metal tables.

Someone called Trace's name and he dodged into view, looking frazzled. His dark eyes were haunted, but his horns perked up to see her. "My beautiful queen, I am pleased that you yet live."

She could barely stop grinning long enough to make an intelligent reply. "I have been told that by my brothers as well. How are you, my heart?"

Grabbing the side of the viewer with one large hand, his expression turned pinched. "I am pleased to be running supplies, rather than warming another queen's bed. If only I were with you once again, all would be well, my queen."

"Our two ships are in route to one another even as we speak. I promise that you will spend this night in my good company."

A smile curved at his lips. "Did you perform the rite of ascension again?"

"Alas, I am unascended. Do you still wish me as your queen?"

Shock tore through his expression. "I wish it, but do not think we will live long enough to enjoy it, my queen."

Feeling put off by his tone and lack of support, Tela stepped back. "Do you doubt my abilities as a queen?"

Shaking his head, his horns slipped back in the traditional display of submission. "Not at all, my queen. Where you lead, I will gladly follow."

Releasing a relieved breath, she tucked her wings neatly behind her back and nodded. "Good. I wish you out of the kitchens this moment. You will prepare a space for us and gather intel just as you did before. Link with my brothers, for they have pertinent information to share with you about my journey so far."

"All will be as you say, my queen." When he pulled back, she spoke again. "Remember something, Trace. You were, are, and will always be first and foremost in my affections. Never for one moment doubt my feelings for you."

The young breeder's handsome face relaxed. That's when she realized that he'd aged about ten seasons in the few weeks they'd been apart. "I must admit that being without you after knowing your tenderness has been difficult. Being at your side will make me whole once again."

"Once we are together, nothing will separate us ever again."

"From your lips to the goddess' ears, my heart."

The moment the screen went blank a deep voice sounded from the security console. "You do not speak or act like a Draconian queen."

When her head snapped over to look at the older warrior, his eyes fell submissively to the floor.

"You heard what happened in the cave of ascension. Think about it. Bridge officers are culled from the smartest and most capable warriors. Security officers in particular are chosen for their analytical abilities as well as their fierceness in battle. If you analyze our situation properly, I think you'll find that I'm the only true Draconian queen in the fleet. My mind and my heart do the talking for me, not some filthy parasite."

Stepping back to look from one crew member to the other, she continued, "Unlike the parasites who rule our sector of space, the human queen and I will not fight each other for dominance, force your loyalty through terror, or kill you if you fail a task. We would never reap our own young or torment males for the sadistic pleasure of seeing them suffer."

Jerking her wings back in frustration, she lifted her chin defiantly. "We see males as worthy of respect. It is up to you to determine who you wish to devote your lives to serving. If you do not wish to stay and fight, we will leave you on a nearby world with a distress beacon. If you choose to stay, know this: We will not tolerate insurrection. The human queen and I have formed an alliance and I'll abide no dissention in the ranks."

Looking around, she saw the males' expressions had morphed into indulgent smiles. Seeing a young female spouting off like a stern queen must be a novelty. Though she should be ecstatic that they were inclined to accept her rule, Tela found irritation churning in her gut. Taking a few easy strides to her chair, she sat down with a thump. "I am not weak," she announced to no one in particular.

Gentle chirping laughter sounded off around the room.

Steepling her fingers together in front of her diminutive body, Tela began to plot her next move. Let the entire 'verse underestimate her if they were so inclined. They'd soon learn by her actions just how formidable she could be. With the *Delacroy* firmly under her feet and her brothers and crew at her side, she'd be in a position to execute battle plans more effectively.

Queen Cassandra was also correct about two ships working together in battle being more effective. Draconian queens had no natural enemies in this sector; they often jostled for power and squabbled amongst themselves, warring with an occasional interloper. Therefore they were not taught battle strategy involving teamwork of any sort. Solo victory was the only honorable way to fight among the queens. That was their one weakness. Planning ways to exploit that weakness became her all-consuming quest.

9 BETRAYAL

CASSANDRA

Cassandra and Mathadar pulled back from the view screen and stared blankly at each other for a brief moment. Their clandestine spying had revealed shocking information that neither of them was expecting. It was a lot to take in all at once.

Shock shot through Cassandra's chest, almost stealing her breath away. "It was clever of you to set up a fail-safe workaround that triggers in the event the doors to the bridge are locked."

"It was in case we'd missed a lone reptilian and he retook the bridge. I never thought it would be triggered by our own warriors."

Bringing up one hand to rub her sternum, she shook her head in amazement. "I honestly never thought Tela would do something like this."

"Like what?"

"Usurp my authority and take charge of this ship, of course."

The commander snorted a laugh. "Then you haven't been paying attention. She is a Draconian queen, raised to wield power over her environment. Expecting her to sit back and do nothing when she has a chance to commandeer her ship is to greatly underestimate her character."

She sighed. "I suppose you're right. At least the other ship hasn't been assigned a queen, so we'll be getting some extra firepower without a fight."

"I suspect the weapons have been pared down. My people do not trust warriors with full armaments."

"Are they suspicious warriors will turn the weapons on them in some kind of uprising?"

"I highly doubt it. They likely see leaving weapons on a vessel they've reassigned to transport cargo as wasteful."

Cassandra thought over the commander's words. "It's a shame, because we could have really used a fully functional vessel. Do you think Tela is really ready for her own ship? Sometimes she seems so young and carefree, but every now and then I get a glimpse that she's restless and eager to have the life she always assumed would be hers."

"She's a young queen and this is a critical time in her life," Mathadar responded smoothly. "If not for her young body expelling the parasites, she would be in command of her own vessel even as we speak."

"Would be, hell, she's in charge of a vessel right now—ours to be precise."

Reaching out to touch her face, Mathadar almost smiled. "You mean *your* ship, my queen. I am but your consort on this wonderful adventure."

Sitting back in her seat, Cassandra mulled over their situation. "Do you think what she said about the others is true?"

"About all the queens being infected with parasites? Though it seems like a mythical story of old, I'm afraid it is likely the truth. Her report to her hatch mates explains far too many elements of our society to be false information."

"We've got to get a real ship under us with enough weapons and crew to fight our way out of this sector."

"Warriors can only function if there is a queen aboard their vessel to lead. Since there are only two awakened queens, we are limited to two ships. I can guarantee it will not be enough."

"Is there any way to get our hands on more unascended queens?"

"I dare say the few that failed in the right of ascension are dead or have been carried off by slavers." Pausing for a moment, he bolted up. "I might know a way to convince young queens to join us before their rites. There are families with a young queen in their midst. If I speak with the males perhaps we can convince some to defect along with their young queen. It's risky, but warriors have long had secret communications we use from time to time to move our sons to choice assignments. I will not be able to contact every vessel because the technology we use must be primitive to escape the notice of our queens. Unfortunately it also has limited range."

Cassie nodded. "If we show the images that we just captured of Tela speaking with her brothers, they may be convinced to remove their daughters away from their parasite-infested mothers. If not, perhaps males will defect to join our cause. The more ships we have, the greater our probability for success will be."

"You are correct." Mathadar's voice became tight with emotion. "Might I suggest we ask the healers to research our medical database in an effort to discover more about the parasites? Perhaps we can develop a biological weapon to use against them. It grieves me deeply to leave our young females to their mercy."

Cassandra felt her chest tighten once again. Reaching out to him, she grasped his hands. "If we could figure out a way to accomplish it, I would destroy that cave and every single parasite sheltered there."

For once when she stared into his eyes, he didn't look away. "It pleases me that your thoughts are the same as my own on the matter. However, I must point out that the Draconian home world is extremely well protected. I do not believe we could get within a hundred parsecs of it. If we managed to land it would a suicide mission because the queens would never allow us to leave again. The best we can do is save as many as we can and live to fight another day."

Reaching out to place her hand over his, she murmured, "Agreed. I don't know if I ever thanked you properly for saving me from the auction block."

His gaze turned warm. "You have thanked me verbally several times." With his next words his expression tightened and his eyes slid away. "Such gracious behavior toward a warrior is unheard of among our queens. Our service is seen as a duty-owed and none acknowledge our sacrifices. They motivate us by using pain and are not forgiving of failure."

Cassandra's throat closed up as she looked at the commander's many scars. It would be easy to feel pity for this man and the others like him who'd apparently had a life filled with pain and virtually no hope of a better life. Yet he was strong and unflinching in carrying out what he perceived to be his duty. Her hands tightened on his. "May I hold you?"

His eyes flew up to hers and his wings fluttered slightly as though startled. When his handsome face creased into an expression of confusion, Cassandra clarified, "I want to put my arms around you and hold you close. Humans call it a hug."

Scooting closer, he dropped to his knees in front of her. Cassandra spread her legs to make room for the bulky warrior and wrapped her arms around his neck, pulling him close. He nuzzled his face into the side of her neck a second before his gigantic arms came around her. "I'm glad to have you at my side," she whispered.

"I would face the wrath of the gods to see you safely back to your own sector of space, my queen."

Grasping him more tightly, she smoothed the back of his neck with her thumb. "I know you probably don't believe me, but I'd give my life to have you all returned to safety as well."

His hand moved up to grasp her hair and he pulled back to look into her face. His gaze became admiring and slightly heated. "When we're together, I can almost believe we have a chance at surviving this. I wish our queens were more like you."

"Unless I miss my bet, they probably are. It's the parasites controlling them that are the problem."

Shock registered on his face for a split second before he gave a slight jerky nod. "It is finally sinking in. They are much like Tela before they ascend."

"Tela seems nice enough." Pulling back, she grinned. "You know, except this whole commandeering our ship thing. Besides that, she's been warm, funny, and respectful of the warriors."

"We've always watched them start out happy and mentally stable, and then they slowly turn toward madness. Now we know why that happens and I am furious. How did they keep that from our healers? Surely scans would pick up the presence of a parasite."

Cassandra rubbed his arm soothingly, even though the grip on her hair had tightened to the point of pain. "I suspect they manipulated the equipment or came up with some explanation for the unusual readings. You said yourself; males never question what they are taught by the females on your world."

"What you say must be true. The parasites evolved along with my people. Since ancient times they were there, behind the scenes controlling and manipulating our society. I long suspected something was wrong, but I never once imagined it was something like this."

"This is bizarrely out of the ordinary and the parasites went out of their way to ensure no hint of their secret got out."

"I fear if they discover we know of the parasites, they will come at us full force to keep their secret safe."

Sliding her hand up to cup the back of his head, she pulled him closer. Staring at his full lips, she tried to stay on task. "We need to alert as many warriors as possible. There's safety in numbers."

His eyes dropped from her eyes to her lips and back again. "You look at me with hunger, my queen." His voice was low, raw, and slightly breathless.

A flutter of wings drew their notice to the far wall. The guards who always followed her were subtly making their presence known. Peering over at them, she asked curiously, "Are they afraid I'm going to kiss you or something?"

"We do not know this 'kess' you speak of. It is their duty to remind you that I am unfit to breed with."

"How's about they let me decide who I want to focus on?"

"They mean no disrespect. You are human and are unacquainted with our ways."

"I'm more interested in your thoughts on the matter, Commander. What do you think of hooking up with a human queen?"

His gaze raked over her, as hot and needy as her own. "This is supposed to be your time of resting."

Cassandra moved closer, maintaining eye contact. "That's not the warmest response I've ever gotten from a man."

There was more rustling of wings near the door. "Responding positively to your question would be seen as seeking the favor of a queen."

Cassandra ignored the guards, pulling him close again.

He swallowed thickly and his voice dropped to a mere whisper. "We know not what the future holds, my queen. Better that you rest now and be refreshed for battle than breed and us both be depleted if we're attacked."

"Humans have a saying. If you don't make time for the important things, you'll never have time for them."

Leaning closer still, he murmured, "Far be it for a simple warrior to disregard the wishes of a queen, especially one such as yourself."

Their new queen tilted her head and ghosted her lips gently over his. It was the sweetest and most intimate display Mathadar could imagine a queen making to a warrior. Something warm and possessive bloomed in his chest, causing him to sink his fingers into her soft skin slightly.

Suddenly, the thought of other warriors seeing her touch him annoyed him greatly. His wings unfurled behind him, blocking their touching from the view of the other warriors. It was a brazenly inappropriate move and one that apparently shocked the guards into silence.

His queen moved forward into his arms. Mathadar sat back, pulling her into his lap. Her legs came up around either side of his hips and her soft breasts pressed into his chest. Images of them naked with skin pressed against skin flashed through his mind.

If he'd thought growing hard between her soft thighs would be off-putting for the small queen, he'd be wrong. Her core moved against his cock, as she took the pleasure she wanted from him. The very same pleasure he was eager to give. The room grew deathly quiet, the only sound he heard was the whisper of their bodies moving together. Even the warriors now understood the diminutive queen would unapologetically take what she wanted from him.

Before she could find her release the entire ship shook as the sound of cannon fire crashed against the outside of the hull. They were under attack, but from whom he couldn't imagine. There was no way their former queen could have caught up with them already, and Tela's training ship was still parsecs away. Untangling herself from his lap, Queen Cassandra staggered to stand up. Coming gracefully to his feet, Mathadar moved his cock to the side and grabbed her hand. They made for the bridge at breakneck speed.

10 AMBUSHED

CASSANDRA

Skidding to a stop when the bridge doors opened, Cassandra collided with Mathadar. The big hunk moved his body slightly forward to absorb the impact. The commander stepped to the side to speak with his security officer as they tracked information on a small console. Gazing at the huge ship eating up the space between them, Cassandra gasped. "Tela, what did you do?"

"The communication with my vessel was interrupted. I don't know how because I was careful to use a full encryption sequence."

"Well, they're sure furious about something. We're no match for a fully armed Draconian warship."

Tela flew from the captain's chair to make room for Mathadar just as another round of cannon fire hit their ship. Tela grabbed the sturdy railing a few feet away to keep herself upright. Mercifully the shields held.

Mathadar's arm came out to steady his newfound love as his forceful voice shouted commands. "Bring up about and down. They've got no weapons underneath their ship."

The navigational officer, Direk, grumbled. "No, but

they'll launch fighters. We won't last long in a firefight with them."

The security officer responded quickly. "Hearing your secret communication with your brothers with their own ears has thrown the crew of the *Falcore* into chaos. I sent a clandestine message to the elders. Even now they are arguing amongst themselves about mutinying against their queen."

"They would never do such a thing!" Direk gasped.

Cassandra dropped down beside Mathadar in the captain's seat. "The hell they wouldn't. Right now Tela is the only true queen in the fleet. They'd take her side over one controlled by a parasite in a heartbeat."

Their security officer shook his head. "They care not for our young Draconian queen, for they do not believe she is any different from the queens we have known."

Cassandra's head shot over to gape at the man. His hands flew over the console even as he spoke. The man's firmly worded addendum was delivered without looking up. "They wish to serve the human queen who they see as different and more worthy of their devotion than any in the fleet."

Bringing her hand to her slowly constricting chest, Cassandra was stunned for a brief moment. They were considering mutiny against a powerful Draconian queen? That didn't make sense. How many warriors were destined to die in that internal conflict? Men were sacrificing themselves to follow her lead when they barely had a fighting chance of survival in the first place. A sick feeling churned in the pit of her stomach at the thought of good men dying.

Mathadar's arm snaked around her back and his hand landed on her hip, in a move that more possessive than protective. He looked down at her with concern stamped on every inch of his handsome face. The things was, she didn't deserve his unwavering support.

Shoving him away, she came to her feet. "Open a communications channel to that ship. I want to talk to the queen."

When the screen lit up, terror tore through Cassandra's chest. This queen was much larger than the one she'd spoken to before. This new queen was almost twice the size of the largest warrior standing beside her. The angry queen's horns were standing straight up, her nostrils were flaring, and a gigantic tail whipped angrily back and forth behind her. Her wingspan was massive. The woman's hand came up and one finger pointed at Cassandra. The claw sitting on her wrist was as large as a human hand. This must be a common gesture among their kind.

"You are to blame for the insurrection aboard my vessel, humon. You will pay dearly for the trouble you caused me this day."

Scurrying to establish a dialogue, lest she be thought foolish or mentally deficit, Cassandra ensured her voice was loud and clear. "Let's just talk about the situation for a minute. There's no need for things to get out of control."

"This is why we do not permit alien queens in our midst. The warriors are so easily led astray, especially when you exploit their desire for better circumstances. Many of them will die today and their blood will be on your hands, humon."

"My name's Cassandra—apparently Queen Cassandra around these parts."

Her hand dropped back down to her side and the Draconian queen assessed her with genuine loathing. "I cannot believe that Heinka let you escape her grasp. She's younger and less experienced than most queens."

"Heinka? I wondered what her name was."

The woman's anger clicked down a notch, her tail stilled, and her hands relaxed. "The only name you need concern yourself with is mine. I am Rovanda of the *Maradox* and I will be the last face you see before you die."

Intent on making herself seem like a worthy adversary, Cassandra quelled the terror growing in her gut and forced some levity into her voice. "It's really cool how Draconian queens always try to psych out their opponents, but that won't work with me." When the woman's expression shifted into one of anger, Cassandra lightened her tone. "Well, Rovanda, when I kick your ass and rip that ship out from under you, I'm going to rename it. I hope you don't mind, but you Draconians suck at naming ships and people."

The woman's mouth fell open in astonishment. "You dare to challenge me? I can take you apart with my bare hands. When you are no more, I will turn my attention to the fallen queen who talks openly about things that should not be discussed."

Rushing to keep the aggressive queen's attention off Tela, Cassandra stepped forward. "You've got a deal. We'll fight face-to-face with no weapons but our fists."

The older woman's eyes lit up. "I wonder how your pain will taste."

Cassandra jerked back like she'd been struck. Her eyes shot to Tela whose tail made a weird flicking motion that seemed almost like a shrug. It communicated she didn't know what Rovanda was talking about. When she looked behind her to Mathadar's face, there was stone-cold fury.

Deciding to leave the bizarre statement alone for now, she turned back to Rovanda, whose expression was something approaching hungry. "Umm, how's about you open your docking ring? You and I will give the warriors a one-on-one battle to remember for all times."

Mimicking her grandiose speech patterns seemed to do the trick. As she'd hoped, Rovanda smiled, showing two rows of sharp teeth. "You are in over your head, little humon. I almost feel pity for you, all alone in a strange sector of space, facing off against a Draconian queen."

"If I'm destined to die, I'd prefer that it be standing on my feet, fighting for what I believe in."

"Weak beings do not have the luxury of standing for their beliefs. The weak cower before the might of the strong. That is the way of the 'verse, you foolish creature."

"Where I come from the strong protect the weak and the weak find other ways to contribute to society. I'm guessing a system like ours wouldn't hold much interest for someone like you, since you wouldn't be in a position to ... taste everyone's pain."

The older queen didn't like having her thoughtlessly spoken words thrown back in her face. Her face darkened and her voice turned menacing. "You should have run when you had the chance, humon. There is no glory in being torn apart by an invincible enemy."

"I'll remind you of that when you're lying bloodied on the floor gasping for your last breath. Perhaps it will be my turn to taste *your* pain."

The woman didn't have a brow, more like a ridge running across both eyes. It creased in a manner that made Cassandra think it was a deep frown. "Humons are arrogant creatures to have such weak and defenseless bodies."

Taking a step closer to the screen, Cassie lifted her chin. "You're focusing on all the wrong attributes, and it's going to cost you in this challenge."

Rovanda turned to one of her warriors. Motioning to

him with one hand, they watched him punch some buttons on a nearby console before murmuring, "The docking ring is open, my queen."

"I will see you on the battlefield, humon." Rovanda spun on her heel and stalked off as the screen went blank.

Tela's serious voice filled the silence that had spun out following her conversation with Rovanda. "You cannot sacrifice yourself for no reason, Cassie. It is not logical. The moment she kills you, she will cleanse this ship of warriors and take her time killing me."

"She can't do that unless you're foolish enough to stick around," Cassandra shot back.

Moving to stand in front of her, Tela asked curiously, "Do you have a plan?"

"Oh hell no, not yet anyway. I'm working on one though."

Tela's horns drooped. "That does not sound promising."

"Look, when I board the *Maradox*, I'll seal the docking ring behind me. I want you to disengage and make a run for your training ship the moment that ring closes. At least you'll be temporarily free of this situation and have two ships at your disposal."

"I do not like this plan of yours, human. We agreed to stand together and fight or die together, remember?"

"Of course I remember. Don't worry about me. I have no intention of dying heroically today. Mathadar and I will figure a way out of this situation."

"He cannot help you in battle. Queens face off in single combat, just as you have vowed to Queen Rovanda."

Pure aggravation fired in her gut at the reminder of her hastily spoken words. "I know what I said."

"Then I should stay and challenge her after you die.

She will be weakened and perhaps I can defeat her if I am fast and clever."

"I appreciate that you want to stick together, but let's face facts. Neither of us could defeat her in single combat, even on our best day. We need to be smart. Our first priority is to rendezvous with your ship. We'll need your warriors to help fight off the other queens when the time comes. You're needed at the helm of your own ship. Your males are counting on you and so am I."

Tela thought over her words and her wings slowly constricted into a tight formation behind her young body. Cassandra was slowly coming to recognize Draconian body language. Tela's tense stance, the upward slant of her small delicate horns, and the fact that her tail was low and close to her body indicated that she was anxious and deep in thought. "Fine, but I will return to your side as soon as possible."

Though Tela's insistence on returning as soon as possible didn't coincide with the half-assed plan Cassandra was forming in her own mind, it would have to do. Reaching out to take both of Tela's hands, Cassandra gave her a word of warning. "Disengage immediately and head directly for your ship. Maintain silence on the communication channels and assign someone you can trust to captain this ship when you board *Delacroy*. Don't take any chances and whatever you do, don't engage with any of the other queens."

Tela glared at her. "I'm not stupid or weak."

"I never for a moment thought you were. I just want you to have the highest probability of success on this important mission. We need both of those ships and any other vessels we can get our hands on."

"Agreed. You can count on me and my brother spawn to complete the mission."

Turning on her heel, she walked over to the captain's chair and waited for Mathadar to vacate it. When he stood there was a slight pause before he walked off. The look that passed between them was grave. Tela straightened her shoulders and sat down, before scrolling going through data on the arm pad.

Mathadar drew her toward the door. The last thing Cassandra saw when the door closed between them and the lift was Tela's back and the faces of five very anxious members of the bridge crew. Mathadar whispered, "We must prepare, for we will be locking onto their docking ring shortly."

"What are my chances in single combat?"

"Do not ask questions you do not wish to hear the answer to, my queen."

"Damn, I thought you were going to say something like that. I guess it's time to get real."

The lift doors opened and several warriors joined them as they moved through the ship, each with an equally grim look on his face. They stopped by several huge metal cabinets in one of the loading bays, and the males began enhancing their armor.

No one spoke as they clicked each new piece into place. The atmosphere led Cassandra to think that they honestly didn't have a chance against a fully-grown, battle-ready Draconian queen.

Mathadar selected pieces of smaller armor and began fitting it to her tiny form. Suddenly, it hit her hard and fast that they were using armor designed for adolescents on her. Tears stung in the back of her eyes. "Your queens send boys into battle as well as men?"

"If it were not so, we would have no need for battle

armor of this size. When there is battle, every warrior is used according to his strength."

"I hate everything about those parasites. Just when I think they can't do anything to shock me, something else catches my notice."

Mathadar began placing weapons all over his body and around her waist. Without looking up, he murmured, "Our lives have been difficult to bear. Because of you, we now have hope of a better life."

"You know we're going to have to fire on her together, don't you?"

"I do know this. Turning our weapons on a Draconian queen is considered high treason among our people. Even if we are victorious and you rule, no Draconian male will ever forget this day. Our actions will make us instantly infamous in this sector. Every queen with a ship will seek the honor of destroying us."

"Hey, why don't we just take on one problem at a time?"

"All will be as you say, my precious queen."

Cassandra stepped into his personal space, tugging him down for a quick kiss. When he pulled back his eyes were glowing with warmth. "Do not leave the circle of our protection. When the battle begins, take shelter behind me. My armor is thicker than yours and my body can sustain more abuse."

"I don't want you to sustain any more abuse. I felt awful when you were injured the first time."

Ignoring her complaints, he continued, "If we all fire at once, perhaps we can penetrate her shield. It is much stronger than the ones afforded to warriors."

"Yeah, they would leave you all with inferior shielding on the off chance it might give them an advantage in a situation like this." Looking around at the nine warriors, her lips pressed into a firm line. "The moment the docking ring closes, surround her and open fire. Don't wait for anything. If we catch her off-guard, we might have a chance."

They nodded as Mathadar clipped a long, thin piece of metal to her hip and a personal shield to her neckline. "Use your shield if all else fails," he whispered. "You can run and hide if we all fall. The shield may not protect you from her specialized weapons, but it will protect you from their scans. If we all die in this battle, it will buy you some time until Tela can return with her brethren."

"You aren't going to fall. Ten of us are going in and I want to see all ten of us standing when she's dead. If we run into trouble, try to get to the control panel and vent them all into space. I know they're wearing protective armor, so they won't die."

"But it will give you control of the vessel." Mathadar's voice sounded proud. "You think of clever battle tactics that no warrior would ever consider using against a queen."

"Women can be devious, especially human ones."

"This I already know."

Jumping onto her toes, she gave him a quick kiss again. The docking ring began to move and within seconds the metal parted to reveal the loading bay on the *Maradox*.

The dominating Draconian queen stood on the far side of the room, straining to catch her first glimpse of her opponent. The moment she caught sight of Cassandra, she snorted a wheezing laugh. Taking that as a bad omen, Cassandra did the only thing she could. She headed for the docking ring, pausing briefly before stepping over the threshold.

Everything about this situation seemed wrong to the conflicted warrior. Turning on a queen was something Mathadar never thought he would consider for a single moment. Honorable males submitted to their queens and their service was marked with self-sacrifice. Yet here he was, preparing to kill a Draconian queen. In truth, he had no choice. Allowing Cassandra to be tortured by the older queen was unthinkable.

His new queen clung to his side, seeking his protection. She'd made the mating gesture to him and asked his opinion on all things large and small. Though he wasn't quite crazy enough to believe she saw him as an equal, it was clear she valued his contribution to the mission and trusted him with her life. It was time to prove that her trust in him was not misplaced. She'd make it through this battle with not so much as a scratch on her creamy soft skin if he had anything to say about it.

Mathadar stepped out in front of her and moved forward with the small human queen at his back. The other warriors spilled out around the room the moment they stepped through the docking ring. His keen senses heard the metal against metal scrape of the ring closing again, trapping them with the oversized Draconian queen.

The look of joy glittering in Rovanda's eyes was familiar. He'd seen the same look on her face as she'd reaped her young while still in the shell right in front of their sires. The same sadistic look was in her eyes when she dug her nail brutally into his shoulder, delving into the joint. She'd worn the same expression when she ordered the ship to jump into hyper-drive while members of the crew were still making minor repairs to the exterior, burning them to a cinder.

The pleasure she took in inflicting pain on her warriors had never made any sense to him, until now. The parasites were likely to blame. Though he knew not the exact reason, he knew the tiny creatures seemed to enjoy viewing the misery of others. Steeling himself for the coming battle, he vowed not to allow Rovanda to touch his new queen's delicate frame.

"Mathadar, you were always the least among our warriors. Why Heinka made you a commander I will never know. It was clearly poor judgment on her part." Her dark eyes drifted from the commander to the woman peering around his shoulder. "No hiding behind your warrior, tiny queen. Now you must back up your brave words with action."

Cassandra stepped forward to stand beside Mathadar. "I'll give you one chance to surrender. You don't have to die today."

Rovanda threw back her hairless head and laughed. "Oh Mathadar, it is a rare treat you bring to me today. Though defeating such a weak opponent will prove to be no challenge, I will delight in peeling her skin from her body one strip at a time."

Raising his laser rifle, Mathadar began bombarding her with shot after shot of laser fire. None of the crew who came aboard joined him in firing upon the massive queen. That should not have surprised him, since they'd been trained from birth to obey and worship their queens.

Her expression shifted from playful to shocked for a brief moment, before turning furious. "You dare to fire on me? Our shielding is designed to protect us from anything a warrior can throw at us."

Mathadar knew his only hope was to overwhelm her shield before she made her way across the room. He tossed aside the weapon and pulled another from his back. Pulling the lever over and over again with one hand, he jerked out a laser pistol and began unloading it at the same time. Thankfully, Cassandra pulled out two of the smaller pistols he'd strapped to her waist and joined him in trying to bring Rovanda's shield down.

Rather than fearful, Rovanda simply seemed furious. Stalking across the large loading bay, she knocked Mathadar aside with one swipe of her hand, cutting a swath across his shield that sparked brightly as he fell back. Pulling a strange weapon from her belt, she brought his shield down with one shot and left a gaping hole in his hip with the next.

"I'll take care of you later." A quick flick of her thumb and she set the weapon to stun. It took three shots to render him immobile.

He watched wide-eyed as Rovanda turned her attention to Cassandra. Bearing down on her, the Draconian queen reached down to grab her with one massive hand. "You will die badly for daring to challenge me." Cassandra ducked and rolled away. Instead of engaging with the queen right away, she scampered to Mathadar's side. Kneeling over him, she was relieved when she saw he wasn't dead. She turned and unloaded both her weapons into the queen's shield. Her best effort didn't even cause a spark.

A malevolent smile jumped onto the woman's face as Cassandra pulled another weapon from his body and began firing again.

Rovanda's voice rang out, "You cannot possibly defeat me, no matter how many shots you fire from your weak weapons."

This was it. She was within striking distance of Cassandra again and there was nothing Mathadar could do about it. His chest constricted as he realized why the other warriors had not joined the fight. The few that were now in his field of vision were surrounded by Rovanda's crewmembers.

As all hope drained from his brain the bay door opened and a large, handsome male skidded to a stop just inside the doorway. He was one of Rovanda's breeders. When the man lifted his hand, Mathadar saw he was carrying a strange weapon similar to the one that had rendered him useless in battle. Laying hands on a queen's personal weapon was considered high treason. Every Draconian knew this. It was one of their most fundamental laws and breaking it was punishable by death.

Rovanda staggered back. "Pern, how could you turn on your own queen?"

"You reaped my young while they were still in the shell. Today vengeance is mine."

Without hesitation, he shot her in the chest several times, causing her shield to drop. Instead of dealing her a death blow, his eyes lifted to the catwalk above, where an equally impressive male stood with a stun gun. Before she could speak, he shot her in the neck, then in the shoulder, and finally in the leg. She made a vain grab for the com unit on her shoulder but her hands were already turning to lead. She took a step and then another before falling to her knees. Collapsing forward onto her hands, she gritted out, "You fight without honor," before falling onto her face.

His new queen turned and began seeing to his wounds almost immediately. "My God, that looks bad." Turning to the crowd of warriors gaping at their defeated queen, she shouted. "Medic. Get a medic."

Two healers rushed forward. One stopped to place Rovanda's body in stasis, while the other ran over to examine his wounds. For his part Mathadar couldn't take his eyes off Cassandra, the one person who'd stepped up to fight by his side today.

A hypo spray pressed against his neck and whatever the healer injected allowed him to move again. Besides the searing pain emanating from the wound on his hip, he felt fine. He reached out to grab Cassandra. "You must move this ship. If others find out you defeated Rovanda they will come for you. Call Sparn to the captain's chair."

Frowning down at him, her mouth moved. "Sparn, I need you."

Sparn was one of the warriors who came with them today. He was trustworthy and would ensure nothing happened to his queen while they repaired his wounds.

His longtime friend muscled his way past the other warriors and dropped down onto one knee in front of their new queen. "I am ready to serve, my queen."

Reaching out to grasp Sparn's shoulder, she gave brief commands. "I want you on the bridge. Maintain silence of the communications channels and set a course to rendezvous with Tela. If we're lucky, the other queens in the sector will think Rovanda defeated me and is going to challenge Tela."

"All will be as you say, my queen. You must lay claim to the warriors aboard this vessel, so they know you are their new queen."

Coming gracefully to her feet, she followed Sparn over to a computer console. He activated the internal com unit and waited for her to speak. Glancing over her shoulder at Mathadar, Cassandra squared her shoulders and focused on the task at hand.

"Attention all warriors. My name is Cassandra of the *Maradox*. I hereby lay claim to this ship and all the warriors on board." She closed her eyes for a brief moment like laying claim to what was rightfully hers was physically painful.

Swallowing thickly, she continued in a solemn tone. "Human queens are nothing like the queens you have known. We don't rule, we lead. Warriors follow only if it pleases them. When the coming battle is over, each warrior must search his soul to determine if he wants to take a chance at a new and better life or if he'd just as soon continue as before. If you don't want to be part of our crew, we'll drop you off on a nearby planet. If you chose to stay, know we expect you to put your best effort into building a new life for yourselves."

Seeking out Mathadar's eyes again, he nodded, encouraging her to continue.

"Right now we will be rendezvousing with Teladora of the *Delacroy*. She is our closest ally and you will treat her words as my own. She's the only Draconian queen in your current chain of command. I would request that you all continue in the positions your former queen assigned for now. If there are problems, bring them to Sparn. I'm putting him in charge of this ship for the next few hours."

Slamming her hand down on the com button, she turned and fast-walked back over to Mathadar.

He reached for her, even as the healer ran a scanner over his wound. "You did well, my queen."

Bringing her hand up to wipe blood from his face, she murmured, "We just need to get through this." Before she could finish, they heard a commotion on the other side of the bay, near the door. Several warriors had tackled Rovanda's breeder and wrestled her weapon from his hands. Whether he had attempted to turn the gun on Cassandra or himself was unclear in Mathadar's mind, but his wing came out to wrap protectively around her small body.

Cassandra turned to look at the healer, who hadn't paused in his assessment. "What is wrong with the one she called Pern?"

The second healer came to assist as the first attempted to explain. "He has been through much with our former queen. It has damaged his mind." Growing quiet for a moment, he offered, "If you wish I can put him out of his misery in a painless manner."

Grabbing the man's arm, Cassandra vehemently shook her head. "I want him someplace safe with someone appointed to look after him for now."

Looking at her curiously, the healer articulated his words slowly. "Perhaps I did not make myself clear. Pern's mind is damaged. Even Queen Rovanda had stopped engaging his services as a breeder." Pausing, he sighed. "He turned on his own queen."

Cassandra's brow creased into a stubborn expression. "Yeah, I saw that. He said she reaped his young. Where I come from, if you mess with someone's kids they'll turn on you with a vengeance. She deserved what she got in my opinion. Get him sorted into a safe space and see he's well cared for. I'll speak with him once we get through this crisis."

"It will be as you say, my queen. I beg your leave to take our wounded warrior to a medical unit."

"Of course. Commander Mathadar is our priority right now."

"As you wish." The healer's voice was short and clipped.

Cassandra's face crinkled into a frown. Mathadar could tell she was confused, so he said what the healer did not. "You should go rest and let the breeders care for you, my queen. Another battle may be upon us at any moment. We need you refreshed and ready to ..."

Cutting him off, she finished his sentence. "Ready for what? To talk bullshit and get you hurt all over again? That seems to be the only thing I'm really good at." Wringing her hands in her lap, she looked away. His poor human queen was not nearly as strong as she pretended while in front of her Draconian peers.

Reaching out to cover her anxious hands with one of his own, Mathadar spoke soothingly. "Do not disparage the queen I have to respect. You did well this day, my sweet queen."

"I'm a fraud and I almost got you killed. If Pern hadn't saved the day we'd both be dead."

A couple of warriors brought over a hovering platform and began to unfold it. Mathadar rushed to get his words out before they put him on the medical transport unit.

"You were brave, the way you stood your ground against an enemy you had no hope of defeating." Gesturing around the room with one hand, he continued, "Look around you, my fierce queen. We are in awe of the tiny human queen who stood her ground against a vicious enemy four times her size." Bringing her hand up to rest on his chest, he murmured. "As unworthy as I am, you stood over me and did your best to protect me. You are a queen worthy of all the devotion we have misplaced in the queens that came before."

Reaching out to cup the side of her face, he wiped away a long tear that trickled down her cheek. "You shed tears for wounded warriors and place yourself in danger for our sake. That means more than you can possibly know to males who have known so little compassion from a queen."

With the assistance of the medic, Mathadar forced himself to his feet. "There is nowhere you can lead that I will not follow, my sweet queen. I trust you like no other."

She flew to his side and helped him onto the platform. It truly felt like his organs had been damaged. The pain was intense and nauseating, but he did his best to conceal it.

"I'm not going to go hang out with a bunch of breeders and rest up while you're injured. No self-respecting woman would do something like that."

Something about her sternly delivered reprimand warmed his insides. Mathadar held onto her hand when they placed him on the hovering platform. Impulsively, he tugged her down to his side. She leaned over and smoothed her hand over the side of his head, uncaring that the healers were maneuvering the platform out of the bay. "How are you holding up?"

Mathadar suddenly realized that he'd failed his queen twice. He worried that although she was concerned about his injuries, even she would not tolerate his ongoing failure to win in battle. This victory belonged to Rovanda's breeder and none other. Perhaps that would endear him to her in some way. Once she spent time with a real breeder, she'd certainly prefer their company. His gut constricted as he realized their time together was limited.

Bringing his hand up to cover her smaller one, he put on a brave face. "It's just a small wound. I'll be up and moving in a few microns. Do not worry yourself about me, my beautiful queen, for I am a difficult male to kill."

She smiled down at him. "Yea, I'm getting that part. It's one of your best qualities by the way."

Allowing his heart to make him foolish, he replied teasingly, "You have yet to sample all my many qualities. Perhaps some you will like even better than my resiliency in the face of death."

Leaning down to kiss him on the forehead, she whispered, "Get better fast. I can't wait to explore everything about you."

The scent of her feminine body called out to him, as her warmth curled around his. This was as close to heaven as he'd ever been and Mathadar never wanted to leave.

12 SPARE THE CHILDREN

CASSANDRA

Cassandra glared at Sparn. "We don't have another queen. They'll just have to make due."

His doubtful expression was nothing short of infuriating. "I do not believe they can function without a queen on board."

Crossing her arms over her chest, she argued her point. "When we catch up with Tela we'll have three ships and two queens."

He looked taken aback when she made the gesture for quotation marks in the air when she said the word "queen." The man had absolutely no idea what her quotation gesture meant, and being referred to as a queen was beginning to grate on her nerves. Their rigid focus on being told what to do all the time by a woman was nothing short of exhausting. "Look, you're all grown-ass men. Just because you haven't had to make decisions for yourself before doesn't mean you aren't capable of doing so."

"Every warrior requires a queen to lead."

"Trust me, you don't."

"What if we make poor decisions?"

"You can't possibly believe that every decision a woman makes is correct."

"Queens can do no wrong, therefore by definition their decisions are always correct." Catching her doubtful expression, he amended his statement. "At times a queen changes her mind with the emergence of new information, but that does not mean her former decision was wrong. It was the best decision with the limited information she had at that particular moment in time."

"Jesus, are you even listening to yourself? Queens are just people. We zig when we should have zagged all the damn time. You're going to take command of that reptilian vessel when we meet up and I don't want to hear anything else about it."

"It will be as you say, my queen."

Pointing her thumb at her chest, Cassie bit out, "Don't call me that. I'm not your queen. I'm his queen." Sparn's gaze drifted from Cassandra to the warrior she was pointing at.

Mathadar gave him one slight shake of his head as if to negate what she was saying. Her eyes narrowed on the man she was becoming obsessed with as she tried to figure out their unspoken communication. "Just do as our queen asks, Sparn. You know that you shouldn't be arguing with a queen anyway."

The disgruntled warrior frowned but dropped his horns submissively. He took a step back and then another. Three more steps and he was backing out the door.

Cassandra spun around to glare at Mathadar. "What the heck was that all about?"

"You well know every ship has a queen, for it is the way of our kind. I fear we are pushing the warriors out of their comfort zones too quickly. If they are anxious, they will not succeed in battle. We need them to be strong and have their heads together to mount a fight when the time comes."

She dropped down on the edge of his healing platform. Mathadar had spent twenty microns in surgery and a medical laser was now flickering back and forth over his wound, finishing the healing process. He could barely see a scar darkening his skin at this point. His new queen was light and the platform didn't move when she sat.

Her pensive voice sounded off. "Perhaps we could find some way of killing the parasite controlling Rovanda and see if she would be willing to join the fight."

Reaching over, Mathadar grabbed a view screen and his fingers flew over the pad. "The healers have performed a full in-depth scan of Rovanda's body. They had to modify our equipment to home in on the parasites. We discovered they've embedded themselves into her brain tissue. They're also covering her spinal cord and have metastasized in most of her organs. The ones in her brain alone have multiplied to the point that they've replaced 18.7 percent of her brain tissue. The healers have determined that there is no saving the older queens. The parasites are simply too deeply embedded into their bodies."

Shoving the screen aside, he responded tiredly, "Our initial communications were keyed to the reptilian vessel and we can't chance reaching out to the elders again. When we meet with the other two vessels I will dig through our communications to see if we got any responses to our offer regarding sheltering younger unascended queens."

"It would be great if we could scare up some other ships to join our cause."

"I fear that even if other young queens joined our cause, the warriors would be suspicious of their motivations. They trust you because you are not Draconian."

"When I was in the marketplace, they were selling all kinds of species. Many of them appeared intelligent and were female."

Rubbing his chin, Mathadar thought it over. "This is the only situation I can envision in which a female would be more trustworthy for having alien blood in her veins. Every warrior knows only Draconian females are given the opportunity to ascend. That fact alone practically guarantees any alien queen we encounter will be parasite-free."

Pulling the data pad back over, she shoved it in front of Mathadar. "When the chips are down, we do whatever it takes to survive. Let's begin looking for females. Trust me, if it comes down to being sold as a slave or leading a ship into battle, most women would jump at the chance to die with a little dignity."

Frowning, Mathadar started pulling up bulletins from several nearby worlds. "Queens should never be forced to make such choices."

Ignoring his response, Cassandra drifted into a pensive trance. "We've gotten ahold of several of the powerful weapons your queens use and we have Rovanda's shield. What if we start challenging queens for their ships and end up with a small armada?"

"That might keep us alive long enough to find a way back to human space."

"Then that's the plan. We gather ships and alien queens. Have you found any other women for sale?"

His hand stilled over the console and he made a strangled noise that sounded like shock.

Cassandra leaned quickly over the data pad, giving a gasp of surprise as well. The woman on the screen was moving around a large cage. She had long tangled brown hair and brown eyes. Her fingers flexed at her side with dirty jagged nails. She was looking all kinds of rough, yet strangely familiar.

"She looks almost human." Tilting her head to the side, she stared silently at the image filling the view screen. "Her ears are slightly pointed and her eyes are larger than human eyes, but other than that, she looks pretty human to me."

"This creature is not human, but you are correct that she is closely related to your kind. Do you think she can be trusted?"

"There's only one way to find out. We have to find her and talk to her."

"She is being auctioned on a planet that is off our current course by three parsecs. I have never been to Strador Five, but I believe it to be a trading hub of some sort. If we stop to secure her cooperation, we will be late meeting with Tela."

"We need this woman and any others we can free."

"Rovanda's holds are overflowing with riches we can sell. No matter her price, we can afford to make the purchase."

"Well, I'm not okay with that. Where I come from we don't buy sentient beings. I say we drop down, shoot the place up, and take them by force. Maybe the locals will think twice before they sell women like meat on the marketplace again."

"Your will be done, my queen. Our shields will hold against anything but a Draconian queen's weapon, and those weapons will not be found in the hands of slave traders."

"Great. You're staying behind until you're fully healed though, because I'm not risking you again."

Mathadar stilled. His face went blank, like it often had when they first met. He was masking his feelings from her again. Finally, he spoke. "If you do not have confidence in my ability to lead, I understand."

Cassandra was on him in a heartbeat, shoving the screen away. "What in the hell are you talking about? Why do you think that I'd have no confidence in you?"

Her behavior startled him, but he quickly regained his composure. Reaching out, he wrapped one hand around each of her arms. She could see he was still fighting to keep the emotion off his face.

"I have failed you in battle not once, but twice. It is kind of you to allow me to live and that you continue to treat me with respect, but we both know I am not worthy to command."

Her hands came up to grab onto his shirt. She balled her fists into the fabric, tugging him closer. "You didn't fail in battle. We both survived. You used your own body to shield me from Rovanda's wrath. If there's anyone who should feel ashamed, it's me for not saying this sooner." Sliding her hands up to cup his face, she looked him in the eyes. "I'm alive only because you protected me when the danger was high. You took the damage yourself that was meant for me. I'm grateful and more proud of you than you can ever know."

Mathadar blinked once and then hauled her close to his body in a tight hug. Cassandra wrapped her arms around his neck and tried to stay away from the laser still moving slowly back and forth over his hip.

A deep voice sounded off from the doorway. "So, it is true what they say. You are nothing like our queens."

Cassandra looked over her shoulder to see Pern standing in the doorway with a warrior at his side. The other man quickly apologized. "Forgive the intrusion,

Queen Cassandra. Pern insisted upon seeing the commander in person."

Pulling back, Cassandra slid from the platform. "Don't give it a second thought. Pern is not on lockdown. He has right to go anywhere he likes on his own ship."

Pern dipped his head in acknowledgment of her words. The warrior beside him backed up to give him some personal space.

Cassandra cleared her throat. "Do you want to speak to Mathadar privately? If so I can leave and give you some seclusion."

Eyeing her suspiciously, Pern asked, "Do you jest with me, my queen?"

Taken aback, Cassandra tried to figure out what his problem was. "Nope. If I were joking I'd say something like, 'since light travels faster than sound, I might appear bright until you hear me speak.'"

It took him a long moment to process her words.

"It's a science joke," she supplied helpfully.

"I believe this would be considered a child's joke among my people. You are small and jest like a child, yet you are a queen and fight like a warrior. I find this contrast amusing."

"If you like jokes involving kids, I have bunch of those. Here's one of my favorites: An amoeba asked his dad how he was made and his father responded, 'Well, sometimes when a man loves himself ...'" Grinning, she waited for him to get it. When no look of understanding crossed his face, she explained, "On Earth we normally begin that conversation by explaining how when a man and a woman are really in love they make a baby. Amoebas reproduce though cell division. Get it?"

Pern's blank stare turned curious. "On Earth females care for their males?"

Feeling like all kinds of crap, Cassandra realized that would be a totally alien concept for him. Nodding, her voice turned serious. "Human women outnumber males by three or four to one right now. Most of us knew we'd never find a mate and it was a pretty horrible feeling. Our dream was always to find a male and fall in love like our mothers did before men became scarce. All we wanted was a normal life and little ones of our own."

His expression turned almost hopeful. "You do not reap them?"

"Hell no. I honestly never heard of any species doing that before I landed in this neck of the woods ... I mean sector of space."

"It is good that you are easy to talk to and have seen fit to bring up the subject I most wish to speak about."

"I heard that Rovanda reaped all your young. I want you to know how sorry I am that you had to suffer through losing your hatchlings. I also want to personally thank you for standing up to her the way you did. You really saved the day."

"You are grateful to me?"

"Yes. I'd be dead right now if it weren't for you. If I can ever repay the debt, know I'll be more than happy to do whatever you need."

"In that case I have a request. It is the reason I came to seek out the new commander. I've been told he is deep in your affections and thought he might sway you to save the lives of our little ones. Though none of mine survived, our former queen had several breeders and between them, they have almost twenty hatchlings in various stages of maturation. If I have pleased you at all, I beg you to spare their lives."

Cassandra stepped out to face the large male. She

reached out one hand to grasp his shoulder. His eyes flew down to her hand and back up to look her in the face. He looked terrified and rooted in place.

"You don't need to ask for that kind of favor from me. Human women never kill off each other's children. You can tell the others that I forbid anyone to harm the children on this vessel or any other ship under my command. The penalty for hurting a child will be death or banishment."

Pern's knees buckled and he fell forward, wrapping his arms around her waist. He seemed to be trembling, and it broke her heart that the poor man thought he needed to worry about her reaping all the children. She wrapped her arms around his head when he buried his face against her stomach. She smoothed his hair like she would to soothe a child and murmured reassuring things to him until he calmed down.

This whole situation was turning into a gigantic cluster-fuck. What's more, Cassandra felt like she couldn't free herself up from dealing with one crisis after another long enough to be proactive. It was getting to be mentally and physically exhausting.

When Pern got himself together, the warrior accompanying him escorted him back to wherever it was breeders congregated. Cassandra realized that she had absolutely no idea where they went, what kind of accommodations Rovanda had thought was appropriate for the kids, or if they were getting proper food and medical attention. Rubbing her temples, she decided on the spot that she needed to make finding out that kind of information a priority. There just didn't seem to be enough hours in the day for everything that needed doing.

A familiar and reassuring voice called out to her. "Come

my queen, rest in my arms. All will be well until the morning."

"I can't believe we've had to fight a Draconian queen and it wasn't even the one chasing us. Will this nightmare never end?"

Turning, Cassandra flew to his platform and snuggled close to the side that wasn't injured. Mathadar seemed to get that she was totally overwhelmed because he wrapped one massive wing around her whole body and pulled her close.

"We will get through this time of great danger and be all the stronger for it, my queen."

She drew up her feet slightly so no part of her was left uncovered, and forced the ideas and images whirling around in her mind to quiet. Mathadar was making some type of gentle trilling noise that she felt in the back of her neck and along her shoulders. It forced her to relax and before she knew it, she was tumbling off to sleep.

13 UNWANTED COMPETITION

MATHADAR

Flexing his stomach muscles and turning from side to side, Mathadar felt no trace of pain. "Your skills at healing are unmatched. My healer is Pharon and even he's never healed me so quickly."

The healer tried to keep the happiness off his face after receiving such a sincere and enthusiastic compliment. "I am familiar with Pharon. We trained together several times. I am glad to know he still lives and practices the healing arts. Though my specialty is healing battle wounds, his is cloning and repairing organs." Glancing from Mathadar to Cassandra and back again, he added, "Lucky for you that was not required to heal this wound, otherwise your recovery time would have been much longer."

"My queen is anxious to see me on my feet again and you have made it so. Therefore you have my deepest gratitude." Mathadar opened one wing and Cassandra stepped close enough for him to wrap it around her slight form. "See my queen, I am well once more."

Looking up at him, she made the mating gesture again, showing all her square, blunt little teeth. "Great, no more getting yourself shot. I don't think my heart can take seeing you injured again."

"I would die a thousand painful deaths to protect you, my queen," Mathadar replied.

The healer chuckled. "You two are like couples of old, before the parasites invaded our queens. It good to see such relationships are not lost to our kind."

"If we manage to get back to the Naxis the women will be fighting each other to get a little face time with Draconian guys."

The healer smiled indulgently at her. "They may be excited to meet the warriors. However, healers are not high status enough to hope for a female to take notice of us."

"Wrong again, little man. Human women love healers. In our society they're considered an even higher status than soldiers."

The healer made a sound of surprise and dropped down into his chair. The stunned expression on his face warmed Mathadar's soul, but they had other places to be this morning. Though they only got a hundred microns of sleep, it was enough to ensure they were alert again.

Looking down at his queen, he asked, "Are you certain you wish to visit the hatchery?"

"Yep, I want to make sure the little ones have everything they need. I don't want anything bad happening to them on my watch."

"That is commendable, but we should hurry. We are coming up on Strador Five and I wish to be well prepared for our mission."

"Let's make this quick then."

Mathadar led her out of the medical unit through an endless maze of corridors and to a lift that took them to another level before they arrived at a cavernous room. It had dozens of glass-fronted incubators lining the walls. Some of them had small hatchlings or large eggs inside. Several over-sized males stepped forward, blocking her view. They were Rovanda's former breeders and they seemed protective of their young. Cassandra had noticed that breeders were larger, like the queens they served.

Mathadar waved them back and moved her forward to look at the incubation units. She peered into each one, smiling and asking questions about them each in turn. Why did this one have such a short tail and why did that one appear to have no claws? Her questions were such that any warrior could answer. He explained that different biological lines had unique physical and mental attributes. Some Draconians were simply born with imperfections, such as the small one with no claws. He'd been at high risk for reaping. Fortunately, their former queen hadn't gotten around to that yet.

An older male stepped forward, introducing himself as the person in charge of the hatchery. Valden had been in charge of Rovanda's hatchery for many long solars and seemed wary of the new queen.

Cassandra perked up. "Am I allowed to hold any of the little ones?"

The older male shot Mathadar a quick glance before pulling out an older one from its housing for her to hold. The hatchling was wearing only a covering around his privates to keep him from soiling his environment. The little one was suspicious at first, pressing his face into her skin. His kind gathered a lot of information with their olfactory senses, so it was no surprise to Mathadar that the little one was scenting her.

The child quickly determined that she wasn't a threat and began climbing all over her, leaving light claw marks marring her skin. Instead of being angry, his queen laughed and lifted the little one up to peer into his face. He flapped his wings and attempted to lick her in the face. "If I knew the breeders better, I'll bet I could probably match the baby to his papa by sight. This one's adorable. Look, he even has little horns!"

Mathadar noticed the breeders slowly relax. Pern had already spoken with them, so that made it easier to believe once they met her in person. The breeders moved forward and pulled out several more young, showing them off. Mathadar had never met a female so thrilled to spend time with another's young. She enjoyed playing with hatchlings like warriors did, holding each of them and snuggling them to her chest. She cooed and emulated their little chirps. Every moment of her interaction endeared her to him as well as his competition, the other breeders.

It was crystal clear that they were intent on impressing her. It would only be a matter of time before she took others to her. She was honestly encouraging their interest by making the mating gesture to them repeatedly. It annoyed him but there was nothing for it.

She spoke in depth with Valden about needs for the hatchlings. Pern arrived in the middle of that discussion with several of the smaller warriors. Rovanda had been breeding for a good many years and was a prolific.

Cassandra met each young warrior and spent a few moments asking about their lives and if they needed anything. They were fairly tight-lipped, since they'd been trained from birth not only to ask nothing of a queen but to avoid capturing her notice, lest she find them less than perfect and reap them on the spot.

It was a shame the small Draconian warriors were forced to be so fearful of their own mothers. Mathadar had to remind himself that it wasn't the females, but rather the parasites that controlled their every action who were responsible for the whole horrible state of affairs. Even now it was tempting to go to the medical unit and simply turn off Rovanda's stasis unit, killing her before she could even get her eyes open.

To Mathadar's mind, as long as the old queen still breathed, she posed a danger to Queen Cassandra. That didn't sit right with him. Since she couldn't be saved, he would need to eventually broach the subject of what to do with Rovanda. For now he turned his mind to more important tasks.

14 ENDLESS AGE

MATHADAR

When his com unit sounded their approach to Strador Five, he encouraged her to say her farewells and deftly guided her to the loading bay. They met a team of about thirty warriors who were already gearing up for battle. Mathadar carefully geared up as well, and then placed a shield on his new queen and loaded her utility belt with not only Queen Rovanda's weapon but a couple of laser pistols as well.

When he was satisfied there was nothing more he could do to increase her safety, he ushered her into the waiting shuttle. He waved the other two shuttles to exit first. The plan was to find the female and any others they could lay their hands on and have the other two shuttles drop down and gather any women before the shooting started. It was a good plan. One he hoped would work.

As they passed the other warriors, their heads dipped slightly in respect. Among the warriors was where Mathadar felt most comfortable. He strapped them both into a bench seat and listened as the conversation swirled around him. Their queen was ever curious, asking the warriors their names and about their interests like they were individuals instead of insects in a swarm about to outlive their usefulness. They warmed to her, eagerly asking about her home world. Mathadar sensed no pending danger from within. Everything was as it should be as the shuttle exited the loading bay and headed for the planet below.

Within sixty microns, they were walking around the marketplace of a large bustling trade center. Strador Five was a little off the beaten path and in a section of the empire he'd never been. The city was larger and more diverse than any Mathadar had ever seen. He kept close to his queen, continually scoping out the area for any kind of danger. He got some disgusted looks from vendors who never liked Draconian warriors in their space. That was to be expected, since most chafed under the rule of the queens. These poor hapless souls could not know that the lives of warriors were oftentimes much harsher than that of regular citizens.

Ralen's voice whispered over the com, "We found the slaves and you are not going to be happy about what we've found. Meet us at the following coordinates."

Glancing up from his com, Mathadar jerked his chin toward the rising sun. "She is about a hundred paces in that direction. The aquatics have more females than we suspected. Some look human, like you. We must hurry; the bidding has already started."

His new queen picked up the pace, running along beside him to keep up. When they spilled into the auction space, pure chaos broke out. Queen Cassandra shouted, "What's happening?"

Bringing his hand from the com speaker against his ear, he replied, "Word is spreading quickly that renegades are attacking."

Straining to see above the crowd of people rushing around, she responded tersely, "I don't see anyone."

Grabbing her roughly by the arm, Mathadar found his hands didn't quite touch her skin because of the shield she wore. Turning her around, he made sure he had her full attention. Gesturing to his chest with his free hand, he explained, "We are the renegades, my queen. Everyone has heard of how we razed the marketplace of a faraway world to rescue you. They know we've come for the females because they are human."

"That explains why everyone is trying to get the hell out of Dodge."

Laser fire began to sound off around them. Cassandra pulled out two laser pistols and looked around for a female to rescue. "We need to free the women without killing all the aquatics this time. I want to know how they got us to Exion."

"Understood, my queen."

Mathadar shouted into his communications device, even as he took aim for the first time. Before he could get turned around, Cassandra had worked her way over to a stack of crates. She investigated each in turn, looking for females. As per their plan, she began scorching an X into the top of each crate that contained a female. He realized rather quickly that she was marking most of the crates.

Cursing under his breath, he activated the homing beacon to draw the two shuttlecraft tasked with retrieving the females. His warriors converged on the area, which was quickly becoming a ghost town. Thankfully, he was seeing less blood and more stunned aquatics. This was turning out to be the best possible outcome. They were gathering queens and beings who might be able to tell them how to escape the rule of other queens.

Mathadar joined her and together they counted the females. There were close to forty in all and most appeared to be human. Once they saw Cassandra's face through the feeding slots, they shouted for her to free them. She tried to shoot the lock on one, but unfortunately, their crates were impenetrable.

He grabbed her shoulder and pulled her back. The females screamed for her not to leave them. It took both hands to wrestle her back from the crates so they could be loaded onto the shuttles. When they landed, dozens of drones came out, attaching themselves to the crates and lifting them into the air. Warriors shoved them along and into the holds beneath the shuttle. They'd been careful to ensure life support was working in that section. If not, the queens would never survive the short voyage to the ship.

There were more crates than the warriors could manage, so they lifted off and Mathadar had to find the transponder keys to free the remaining eight females. Two of his original crew dragged a barely-conscious aquatic before them.

Cassandra stalked forward and spoke before anyone else could. "Tell me how to unlock the crates and I'll let you go."

The aquatic looked terrified. It was not surprising since the crew decimated the town square. The Draconians allowed no planet to have a standing security force for fear they would turn it against the queens. It made them easy prey.

"I do not know," the male stammered. He was very typical for an aquatic, with gills that could process oxygen both under and above water. Right then his head fin was drooping and he was sweating something slimy.

"I've been taught it is a natural defensive technique that allows them to slip free from their captor's hold," Mathadar said.

Queen Cassandra grabbed his gills, lacing her fingers through the opening. Tugging him toward her, she squeezed until he squealed in pain. "You found a way to my home world. Instead of a nice greeting and establishing trade negotiations like every other alien race, the first thing you do is begin stealing women. Well, no more. All that trafficking in human flesh stops now." Squeezing so hard the slave trader gave another yelp, she gritted out, "You're going to help me put a stop to it, or so help me God, I'm going to end you where you stand."

"Stop! You're ripping my tympanic tissue. I'll tell you what you want to know if you let me go."

Letting go, Cassandra wiped a clear slime onto his shirt. "How do I open the crates?"

Huffing out an exasperated squeak, he turned his body slightly. "Attached to the back of my belt is a DNA sequencer. You scan the cargo and input the sequence into the digital lock."

Snatching the device, Mathadar used it to scan the nearest queen.

"That's real clever. You better pray this works," Cassandra murmured.

"It will. Look, I'm Jarek, the ship's hired cook. I'm a nobody who makes food. Trust me, I'm not interested in putting my life on the line over another man's cargo."

Cassandra punched him in the face. "My people aren't cargo, you turd."

Mathadar frowned, glad one of his warriors had taken the precaution of binding the cook's hands behind his back before bringing him before their queen. The aquatic was nearly twice her size and didn't look truly sorry to Mathadar's eyes.

Finally, the crate popped open and a female came

rolling out. Getting to her feet, she went straight for Jarek. Cassandra collided with her right before she made contact with the still-bound man. The queens fell to the ground, fighting for dominance.

When they broke apart, the woman snarled. "Let me at him."

Cassandra held up her hands in a placating gesture. "Absolutely not. When the dragon warriors freed me, we made the mistake of killing all the aquatics. We're not doing that again. We need them."

The woman stood up straighter and dusted off her threadbare clothing. Her long stringy hair might have been black at one time but it was matted with so much filth it was difficult to tell. Her black eyes had a slight slant, giving her a slightly different albeit pleasing appearance. Her slim form was emaciated, but she had the same abundance of breasts that distinguished their new queen. Thinking she might be dehydrated, Mathadar immediately removed the small hydration pack from his waist and handed it to her.

She snatched it so fast he hardly saw her move. Tearing it open, she asked, "The dragon guys might be nice, but the fish dudes are total assholes. We don't need them for anything."

"We're stranded in another sector of space light-years from Earth." Gesturing at the gaping aquatic, Cassandra continued. "These idiots are the only ones who know the way back to our galaxy."

"Fine. Get the information and let's go."

"Hold up, honey, I'm the one in charge of this little rescue."

As the queens argued for dominance, Mathadar tossed the DNA scanning device to one of the other warriors and they took turns opening the other cages.

The newly freed woman glared at Cassandra. "Who the hell are you?"

"I'm a big nobody, just like you," their queen shot back hotly. "One minute I was hiking and the next I was on an aquatic ship. I made friends with a dragon girl and we talked the warriors into rescuing us. My name's Cassie Donovan."

The one with matted hair nodded slightly. "My name's Aiko Hara and I'm going to kick that guy's ass if it's the last thing I freakin' do."

"No one's kicking anyone's anything. Like I said before, I'm the one calling the shots. We need to focus on getting home."

"I don't care who's in charge as long as I get to throttle that one when this is all over." Pointing to the one aquatic that happened to be conscious enough to answer questions, she stared him down. "That one gave us total garbage to eat for months."

The man shrugged, smiling nervously. "I never said I was a good cook."

The newly freed queen lunged for him, but another warrior held out his arm to stop her. If the look on her face was any indication, she was going to get her way with the cursed man at some point and Mathadar couldn't say he cared much if she did.

"No one's throttling anyone, until we get back to the Nexis," Cassandra said, her voice turning harsh. "We're not safe here. I have a ship in orbit and we need to get the hell out of here before more Draconians show up."

"I'm not going anywhere without a bath and something decent to eat," the new queen responded defiantly.

"We got all that covered on our ship. Come on, we've gotta get moving."

By that time the few other queens were free and they made a mad dash for the remaining shuttle. The shuttle lifted off before the newly acquired queens were even strapped into their safety harnesses. Space was tight, so Mathadar pulled Cassandra down onto his lap and strapped them in together.

He remained respectfully quiet as the women began to speak. The warriors moved around, ensuring safety harnesses were secured, passing out hydration packets and food bars.

Ralen kneeled beside the angry queen and held out another hydration packet. She took it more gently this time. He held up a food bar and murmured, "I apologize, my queen."

She appeared taken aback. "Say what? I don't understand."

Ralen glanced around before answering. "I apologize for having such unworthy nourishment to offer such a spirited queen."

Turning to Cassandra, she asked, "Is he for real?"

Cassandra smothered back a smile. "I'm afraid so. Draconian warriors think of all women as queens. They're used to a matriarchal society and have been groomed from birth to follow directions given by females. Unfortunately, all their women are infected with some parasite that makes them bat-shit crazy."

Tearing open the food bar, Queen Aiko waved her hand in the air. "Tell us more."

Cassandra tried to reassure them that they were free without frightening them about their circumstances. "This sector is ruled by really vicious Draconian queens. They have a home world and some rite of passage where the young girls walk through a parasite-infested pool. The parasites colonize their brains and bodily organs. We've got one in stasis on our ship and we're trying to figure out how to kill the parasites and save the woman. The queen we have is older and really infested, so we can't really do anything for her."

One of the other queens stopped sipping her hydration pack long enough to ask, "Exactly how far from Earth are we?"

Cassandra sighed. "Near as we can tell, millions of light-years away. It took me years to get here."

Aiko perked up. "They must have found a quicker way, because I was on Earth a few months ago."

"Luckily we didn't kill all the aquatics this time, so maybe we can beat some information out of them."

Rolling her head over to look at the silent cook, Aiko smirked. "Or we could just get him to cook something and force them to keep eating it until they break down and tell us everything."

Queen Cassandra laughed, shaking on Mathadar's lap. "How the hell old are you anyway?"

"Nineteen." Putting her hand over her mouth, she laughed before holding up two fingers. "I'm legal, scout's honor."

"I thought that's something that only Boy Scouts did."

"Well, they've been called Scouts BSA for about fifteen years now. It is the year 2032 after all."

Cassandra jolted forward in his lap. "According to my calculations it's only 2016."

"They must have put you into hyper sleep at some point. Sorry about that."

Mathadar rubbed her back soothingly, trying to console her. "We discussed that possibility. It matters not the date, since you told me that you left no one of importance behind. Am I not right, my queen?"

Turning over her shoulder, she nodded slightly. "I suppose you are right. As long as I have you, I'll be fine."

Pulling her against his chest, he wrapped her long hair around his hand, tugging her head gently back to gaze into her eyes. "There will never be a day when I am not at your side, my lovely queen. Though I am but a simple warrior, I will dedicate myself to seeing to your every need."

He brazenly dipped his head to brush his lips over hers in the human kiss she loved so much. His intent was distracting her from the terrible news that she'd been separated from her people for an endless age. However, once their lips touched, everything else was forgotten.

The other queens' soft voices and sighs sounded off around them, but his queen only pulled him closer, losing herself in his touch. Pride bloomed in his chest that he could please her so easily. Perhaps the next time they were resting together, she would allow him to pleasure her delicate body. Though having such thoughts running through his head was thoroughly inappropriate, he could not force them away.

15 DESERVING OF COMPASSION

CASSANDRA

Lying against Mathadar's chest in the shuttle, Cassandra finally felt the weight of the day pressing down on her. Rushing from one crisis to another had taken its toll all over again. Would there ever be a day when she could just drift along under Mathadar's wing, enjoying his company?

Smiling to herself, Cassandra realized she was thinking of him as her "one." As far as getting to know each other went, she knew all she needed to about the handsome commander. He was everything she could have hoped for in a husband, not that Draconians got married. They called it breeding and their concept involved one queen with a small stable of warriors.

His wing came up more snugly around her as his breath whispered through her hair. She drowsed in the warmth of his arms for about fifteen minutes and was woken when the shuttle docked with the *Maradox*. Stretching, she came to her feet and followed the others out to the loading bay.

The sight she saw tore at her heart. The women were still being removed from the crates. Each time a new one was released several others came to greet her. Some were visibly broken and others were furious, much as Aiko had been. She moved forward to speak to them, assuring them that they were free and safe. Aiko stayed at her side, standing proud and strong. It seemed to give the others hope.

Stopping before a cluster of newcomers, she tried to sound reassuring. "Don't worry, you are free and safe aboard our vessel." Others pressed in to hear her words. "We're really far from Earth, but I'm going to make sure we stay safe. Even if it takes our entire lifetimes, I'm going to make sure we get back home." She was shocked when the assembled women began to react negatively. The look on their faces told her maybe that wasn't such a great idea.

Although none of the women were particularly old, a couple did appear to be in their forties. One of them immediately spoke up. Though her voice was strained, she spoke with a quiet dignity. "Earth has fallen in the years you have been gone."

"When I left, things were bad. We were cleaning Earth's oceans and planting forests. We'd lost a lot of people, but we were making progress. Earth had even made contact with alien species and they were helping rebuild."

The older woman shook her head as others began to whisper. "We lost the battle. We were forced to move underground. We couldn't grow enough food to sustain our numbers."

Cassandra's chest tightened. It was difficult to imagine things getting much worse than they'd been when she was taken. "I was hiking in the Sierra Mountains, pulling soil samples at different elevations to help our science team get a handle on the mounting disaster."

The older woman took a step closer. She was thin and unwell. "They were on the right track. All the low-lying areas withered first, leaving only a few marginally habitable places high in the mountains. Mountain people got one look at the underground cities and most just climbed right back up to their mountains. They eke out a meager existence, coming to the cities mostly for medical care. God only knows what they're eating up there."

"Think dystopian future, only it's happening now," Aiko chimed in calmly. "They say the tipping point happened decades ago and there was nothing we could do."

Wrapping her arms around her waist, Cassandra's stomach churned. "In other words we wasted precious time and resources fighting a battle we couldn't win when we should have been developing underground cities that were big enough to house Earth's entire population."

Aiko sighed. "Maybe we should begin thinking of this ship as our new home. We'll be like vagabonds, traveling the 'verse with no real planet to call home."

Feeling shocked and helpless, Cassandra nodded slightly. "I've not seen enough of our sector of space to know if there are habitable planets for us to resettle on, even if we get back to the Naxis. I hate to think of us trying to make a life for ourselves here in Exion space."

Aiko piped up again. "Yeah, they told us all about how the Draconian queens rule this vast expanse of Exion space."

"We've faced off with a Draconian queen and it's not a fight we can win all on our own. Don't worry, we'll think of something." Since no useful purpose was served by vacillating over their current situation, Cassandra allowed the breeders to break them into small groups. "Right now I need you all to get cleaned up, hydrated, and rested. We don't know what the future holds, so make sure you're ready for anything."

Watching the small clusters of women being fussed over by the breeders made something in her chest loosen. There were at least three or four alien females who were a bit more jumpy than the humans. It was clear they were ill at ease around Draconian warriors.

Mathadar whispered in her ear, "Do not worry over the other females. Breeders are well trained in caring for the needs of queens. They will be cleansed, clothed, and fed before being given a private space to rest. They know we mean them no harm."

Surveying the room more closely, she eyed the aquatics. The warriors had bound them up and they were sitting on the floor off to the side, looking guilty as hell.

"Do we have a space to lock them down in? The last thing we need is for them to be running amok on board our ship."

"The needs of our new queens come first. The females are weakened, dehydrated, and in need of medical care. Those males are the reason for their distress. Therefore, they will remain where they are and bear witness to the wrongs they have committed. When the queens are healed and settled, the remaining warriors will lock them in the Guared."

"Guared? Is that like a holding cell?"

Nodding, he slipped a wing around her. "It is the lowest point in our ship and contains cells very similar to the ones they used to house the queens. The Guared is a fine place for criminals and dishonorable males who think nothing of harming queens."

Cassandra nodded. Every muscle in her body ached and her exhaustion was bone-deep. She retained enough awareness to find the symmetry of the situation ironic. "That's what humans call poetic justice."

"I do not know what that means, my queen, but I think it will serve them well to be placed into the same situation they sought to keep innocent queens in. And while in route to meet with Queen Tela, we will force them to reveal the way to Earth. Once we are in your sector of space, we can scout for a suitable planet to call home."

Leaning back against his warm body, she allowed herself to think over what that would look like. "Can't we scan their brains or something? I don't know if I want them tortured for information. That doesn't feel right to me."

"They harmed queens and are not deserving of our compassion."

"Humans believe in giving compassion, whether it's deserved or not because resorting to violence diminishes both parties."

"I promise that I will do only what is necessary to elicit the information required to keep you and your fellow queens safe. That is as compassionate as I can be to such undeserving males."

"Speaking of people who don't deserve compassion, we need to discuss what to do with Queen Rovanda," she said.

Without stopping to think, Mathadar suggested, "We can destroy her while she sleeps. She will feel no pain."

She blinked and her mouth dropped open. "I suppose we could do that. I would prefer that we leave her on an uninhabited planet where she can't hurt anyone but herself."

"Gods of Chaos, you would prefer exile over death, even for enemies who wished you dead."

Cassandra frowned at him. They'd already been over that.

"I can see that if I have any hope of truly being accepted

by you, I must stop suggesting death as the solution to every problem," he said.

"There are lots of options that don't involve killing. I'm just suggesting that we explore some of them occasionally."

Bowing his head slightly, he murmured, "Your kindness defines you as a person, my queen."

"I'm not sure that would be considered a compliment by most Draconians, my handsome commander."

Fluttering his wings slightly, Mathadar couldn't say he liked that particular endearment. "You still have not settled on an endearment for me have you, my queen?"

"Nope. What do Draconian queens call their one and only true love?"

"In ancient times when we mated one male to one female, the male was called a Takadon. We now use the term to denote a queen's favored breeder because all queens keep a stable of breeders."

"I wish you were my Takadon."

"I thought you were still getting to know me."

"We've been through a lot in a short period of time. You're the one for me. I can feel it all the way down to my bones."

Using his wings to pull her forward against his front, he encouraged her to lay her head against his chest.

"I love this pose because I can hear your heart beating."

He shook slightly with laughter. "You are hearing two hearts and various other organs that humans do not have, my sweet queen."

"I'll have to learn all about Draconian biology, so I'll know what I'm dealing with."

"If you wish to know about my body, it will please me to have you explore all that I have to offer."

She laughed softly. "Are you perchance flirting with me, Commander Mathadar?"

"If I have any hope of becoming your Takadon, I must ensure you know of my many fine qualities."

Turning to fully face him, her hands went up to cup his face. "Where is that reticent warrior with the blank expression that used to be called by your name?"

His eyes lit up with something approximating adoration as he responded quietly. "Something terribly dangerous happened to him." Leaning down to rub his nose along the side of her face, he whispered, "The foolish warrior lost his fear of his new human queen. She's sweet, delicate, and her intoxicating scent is interfering with his ability to think clearly."

Pulling him gently down for a kiss, she nearly forgot that they were out in the open, where other warriors could see. Slipping a wing around her, Mathadar hid their kiss from prying eyes. When his other wing came up, the space they shared felt warm and intimate.

She moved closer and her hands slid innocently down to his hips, one covering the spot where he would one day carry their young. Feeling her hand touching the fabric of his uniform must have reminded him of breeding, because he pulled her closer and his hands ran down her back to cup her ass. It felt like a brief moment of respite from the dangers and worries of the day. Maybe this was what couples did—take comfort in each other's arms when the stress became overwhelming.

16 THE TRUTH HURTS

MATHADAR

Holding the new queen in his arms had triggered a release of pheromones so strong that every warrior in the loading bay had noticed. Mathadar hustled her out of the area, not caring for the heated looks being tossed her way. Warriors would never approach a queen, even a delicious one in heat. They were far too disciplined for that. Therefore, her safety was not at risk. The thing that worried him was the dark, possessive feelings that rose up in soul when all their eyes were on her. Naturally, the aquatics didn't notice a thing because their breeding was different. The dragon in every warrior warmed to her instantly.

Suddenly, nothing mattered except getting her out of the area. Interrogating the aquatics for intel about navigating to her home world would have to wait. His queen had a dreamy expression on her lovely face and allowed him to guide her effortlessly through the ship.

Upon approach to her quarters, the males standing around the area ruffled their wings in annoyance to see him still at her side when there were actual breeders on board.

Crossing the threshold with her at his side felt like winning a race.

"Do you mind if I ask why they flutter their wings like that?"

A deep voice sounded off from the far side of the room. "They do not approve of the commander coming into your quarters when you have breeders to care for your every need."

Mathadar jerked to attention upon seeing two breeders rise from the settee. Queen Rovanda was renowned in the fleet for collecting the largest and most physically impressive breeders. Something about them being in the queen's private chambers made the contrast between them and himself obvious. Mathadar's arms tightened around her for an instant. Shoving his possessive urges back, his arms slid away and he took a step back to give her space to properly consider her situation.

Unable to quite manage the warrior's face he normally wore for stressful situations, his head jerked slightly to the side as he tried to rein in his emotions. His hands fisted and he pulled is wings back tightly behind his bulky frame. Compared to the breeders, he was a miniature version of a male. Breeders were bigger because Draconian queens were grotesquely large and required breeders who were larger and more durable.

White-hot fury filled Mathadar's chest when he felt his opportunity to be her takadon slipping away, perhaps forever. They glared at him, like he shouldn't be at her side. In truth he probably shouldn't, but he desperately wanted to be.

His queen's head spun around to look curiously over her shoulder. "Math, what's going on here?"

Before he could speak, one of the breeders rushed to

explain. "I am Roan and this is Falen. We were Queen Rovanda's most dedicated breeders. When you defeated her and took this vessel we became your property as well."

Cassandra took a staggering step back and her hands went up in a defensive pose. It triggered Mathadar to step forward once again, stopping only when his chest made contact with her body. She moved back slightly, sealing them together. Her voice trembled slightly when she spoke. "What do you mean by 'property'?"

The one who called himself Roan gestured with one hand between them. "I now belong to you. We all do. You defeated our queen in battle, and all that she owned now belongs to you."

Mathadar felt her going slack against him. Thinking quick on his feet, he scooped her up into his arms and walked over to the settee. Though the massive breeders gaped at him, they did not interfere. He settled down with his new queen deposited so close to him that a ray of light would not have shown between their bodies. Wrapping a wing protectively around her, he slid his tail up to rest in her lap. Just as he thought she would, the distraught queen wrapped her hands around it and struggled to regain her composure.

Falen spoke for the first time. His horns were slicked back against his head and his tail appeared to be frozen in place. The handsome caretaker was quietly freaking out. Glancing from Cassandra to Roan, he stated timidly, "I have never seen a queen behave in such a manner when confronted by her breeders. Perhaps we should call for a healer."

"She is well," Mathadar snapped. "Who are you to judge a queen and find her lacking?"

Finally Cassandra sucked in a deep breath and shook

her head as if to regain her clarity of thinking. "Mathadar's right. I'm fine. Now explain more about me owning people, 'cause I don't think that's going to work for me."

At that point even Roan shot Mathadar a helpless look. When he looked down at her, Cassandra tilted her face up to gaze into his eyes. "Draconian queens choose their warriors when they come of age. There are databases full of information on unclaimed warriors. They summon us to them and if they like of us, we are theirs."

"Tela mentioned something about claiming her warriors, but I was under the impression she interviewed them and they mutually decided they were a good fit for her crew." Noting his confused expression, she added, "You know, kind of like a job interview."

"If interviews consist of queens demanding answers and demonstrations of our skills before deciding to remove us from our sires to serve her, then it is the same, my queen."

"What are you saying? Being claimed by a queen separates family units and is a lifetime appointment?"

Pressing his lips into a firm line, Mathadar only now realized how naive his new queen was about Draconian culture. Worry snaked through his gut, for in order to effectively lead, she would need to become familiar with their ways.

"As you well know, our society is ruled by females. They care only for propagating daughters to follow in their wake. Sons are raised exclusively by their fathers."

"You did not know your mother?"

"I knew her by sight and thankfully she'd lost interest in my father when I was small so she never looked in on me. Each time a Draconian queen's eyes land on a young warrior, he risks being judged and found lacking. Weak males are reaped, no matter their age. My father spent most of my childhood keeping me from accidentally crossing her path."

"I don't understand. If she never saw you, how would she know you were her son?"

"Such an innocent question," Roan murmured.

Mathadar brought his hand up under her chin and tipped her head back slightly to get a better look at her delicate features. "Each ship carries only one queen. If her eyes landed on a young warrior, he could be none other than one of her own."

Her eyes misted up. "I'm sorry you had to endure that. On our world sons and daughters are considered equal."

Dropping his hand, Mathadar continued to explain. "Among the Draconians daughters are few and sons are many. We are not valued by our females and only occasionally find favor in their eyes. Our queens are capricious and give no care for our safety or consider our wishes when taking us from our fathers and brothers. They lay claim to whom they wish." Mathadar tried using her human family designations in an effort to help her grasp the magnitude of what he was communicating.

Roan interjected, "If two wish the same breeder there may be a challenge, but no sane queen would squabble with another over plain warriors." Shooting Mathadar a condescending look, he added, "Good breeders are scarce where warriors are plentiful and easy to replace."

Cassandra turned slowly around to look at Roan. There was a long drawn-out pause as she rose to her feet. Mathadar rose to stand behind her once more, his wings unfurled halfway. His tail snaked around her leg in a gesture meant to remind her of words about making him her Takadon. It was a defiant and possessive pose and totally inappropriate, but Mathadar couldn't bring himself to care.

Cassandra's hands landed on her hips. "Let me get this straight. You think I should toss Mathadar aside and share my bed with you instead?"

Taking a respectful step back, Roan was clearly thrown by her serious tone. "I meant no disrespect, my queen. I do not judge queens for their various perversions. My intent was to …"

Their queen made a small noise that communicated anger or frustration. "Stop right there. Did you just call me perverted?"

Looking totally lost, Roan gestured to Mathadar. "You just admitted to having a warrior in your bed."

"It is considered a perversion for queens to breed with common warriors. Associating with warriors is beneath the dignity of a queen in general and that's why breeding with us is considered deviant behavior," Mathadar explained.

"Well, humans are like that. We choose based on the male's character and personality."

Roan clearly did not understand what their new queen was attempting to communicate because he continued attempting to tactfully make his point. "I understand that until you defeated our former queen you did not own breeders, but now you do."

"Humans don't own people."

Falen stepped closer to his friend. "Does that mean we must seek out another queen or will you dispose of us?"

Before she could respond, Mathadar clarified quickly, "Dispose means kill. I do not believe you would wish for the breeders to be harmed since you did not even wish that for our enemies."

Making an imperious slashing gesture with her hand, Cassandra responded quickly, "I don't want to see anyone hurt. I just want them out of our room."

Roan spoke again, growing more alarmed. "If you dismiss us, who will be here to watch over you when things go wrong with your breeding of the warrior?"

"Breeding isn't complicated. I think we can manage."

Falen's timid voice sounded off again. By this time the shy breeder's wings were touching the floor and his expression was totally bewildered. "But who will draw your bath, rub your tired muscles, and polish your delicate claws? Breeders are more than just males who breed. We were trained to care for the bodily needs of a queen."

Cassandra smacked her forehead gently with the palm of one hand. "Now I get it. Being a breeder is a specific job description with assigned duties, only those duties involve ensuring the health and happiness of your queen." Looking at them from one to the other, a smile split her face. "Humans break apart the baby-making process from the caretaking process. We usually only choose one male to breed with and he's more like a life mate that we love and cherish."

"A warrior can only bear two or three hatchlings at a time, but breeders have adapted to spawn up to a dozen at a time."

"Damn, I did not know that. Well, I'm glad I chose Mathadar because I don't know what in the 'verse I would do with a dozen young. Humans co-parent their own children, so I only want what we can manage."

Roan's head tilted to the side slightly. "I see."

"We have special places we go to called spas. The people who work there have your skill set. They wash and cut hair ... polish claws and give body massages."

"They do not breed for the females?" Falen asked cautiously.

"Hell no. At the end of the day they go home to their

own wives and children. It's just their job, not a lifelong designation of some sort."

Roan's facial expression shifted into an almost-smile. "You do not wish us to serve as your breeders and are releasing us to be claimed by other queens. Is this true?"

"No. I'm saying get a backbone. If you see a queen you like, walk up to her, let her know you are attracted to her, and ask her to spend some time getting to know you."

That wiped the smile right off his face. "Males do not pursue queens. It is forbidden."

Cassandra's shoulders dropped and she sighed.

Mathadar peered around her shoulder to look at her face. "Among our kind, queens lead and males follow. Since you are such a deviant queen, perhaps you would wish to establish new rules for breeding human queens."

"What?"

"We are honorable males and therefore we do only what is permitted. However, we wish to behave toward our new queens in a manner that meets their expectations," he said.

Understanding jumped onto her face and she turned back to the breeders. "Human women consider it a high honor to be approached by males. We appreciate compliments and small tokens of affection from males. We don't have self-esteem issues or anything, but being pursued by a male is a strong part of our cultural history."

Roan jerked back slightly. "We are to pursue queens now?'

Giving a wave of one hand, she shrugged. "You don't have to do anything you don't want to do. You can pursue queens, wait for them to pursue you, refuse advances from a queen, or stay happily single. When it comes to humans, we only want to be with people that want us in return."

"This is a new concept for us, Queen Cassandra."

Reaching out, she grabbed Roan lightly by the arm and he allowed her to turn him around toward the door. She got him moving as she spoke. "Great. Think all that over and share it with the other breeders and warriors. Just remember that when you're pursuing a queen, no means no."

"When do you wish us to return for your daily grooming?"

Rushing them along, she responded lightly, "I think it would be a brilliant idea if you opened a spa and invited the women and warriors to come for health treatments. Everyone could mix and mingle in a relaxed setting."

Roan shot Mathadar a quick look and the commander nodded, verifying that she was being sincere about that suggestion. Mathadar watched gleefully as the males he feared would woo away his queen were ushered out the door.

17 A MOMENT IN TIME

MATHADAR

She voice-prompted the lock to engage before spinning around and pressing her back to the door. "I didn't think they were ever going to leave."

Walking up to her, Mathadar cupped her face in his hands. "You shoved two perfectly good breeders out the door and chose to keep me."

"Yea, sorry about that. I hope I wasn't too rude."

His eyes lit up. "You chose me over males that could give you things I can't."

Frowning, she gazed up into his handsome face. "Sure I did. We already discussed all about how I want you to be my Takadon. I sure as hell don't need three."

Mathadar swallowed hard. "You said human women only take one mate and yet you chose me."

Nodding, she asked, "What's gotten into you?"

"I am to be your one and only male, like the queens of old?"

"That's the plan, but only if you want me. If I remember correctly, you never said yes to becoming my Takadon."

"Then I now say yes to you, my beautiful queen. Yes a million times over."

Raising both hands above her head, Cassandra pumped her fists in the air. She was enthusiastically making the mating gesture to him again. He could see every single one of her flat teeth. Mathadar could not be certain, but it seemed as though she wished to fly with him again. He wrapped both arms around her and spread his wings. Her chamber was the largest on the ship. When her feet left the ground, she wrapped them around his waist.

When he saw her biting her bottom lip, it reminded him how it felt to kiss her soft lips. Bending down, he slid his lips over hers and the passion between them flared to life. His tail seemed to have a mind of its own, slipping around to wrap around her waist, gripping her tighter against his bulging cock.

Her soft feminine scent bloomed. Draconian males procreated by a process of parthenogenesis. Their reproductive system was triggered by the saturation of female pheromones, pheromones much like his queen was releasing now.

She whispered in his ear. "I want you."

Pure male pride surged through his mind. Her words coupled with her alluring scent could only mean one thing: She wished to breed him this night. Slowly lowering them to the floor, he kept her in his arms as he made for the sleeping platform in the next room. She was already trying to kick off her boots when he sat her on the bed.

He gladly kneeled at her feet and pulled them off. Stepping back, he watched her tug at the magnetic seam on her uniform, slowly peeling it back from her shoulders, revealing all the creamy flesh he might ever wish to see. He made a trill of surprise. "If I thought you beautiful in your clothing, it was nothing compared to seeing your body bared to my sight."

"Glad you like what you see." Shoving the uniform down her long lithe legs, she kicked it to the floor. "You're stuck with me, now."

Mathadar began tearing at the front of his uniform and kicking off his boots at the same time. His gaze never left his new mate. In fact, he was so busy admiring her slight form, he didn't notice that her eyes were busy drinking in every detail of his body. When his eyes met hers, he stood up and flared his wings out. Standing in formation before a human queen felt strange, but he decided that things were going too well to risk stumbling now.

"Hey big guy, I'm over here and I'm getting tired of waiting for you."

Unable to keep the smile off his face, Mathadar chided himself for thinking even for a second that she would wish to inspect him before mating. That was something only demented Draconian queens did. Moving quickly to the sleeping platform, he gazed down at her, unsure how to proceed.

Huffing out an exasperated laugh, she stated, "You're invited to join me on the bed and touch whatever you like."

That was the all the invitation Mathadar needed. Leaning over, he made the human kiss with her once more. "Umm, you smell really nice."

This time she tangled tongues with him. Her soft tongue sliding over his made his already hard cock throb with need. Bringing up one hand, he wrapped it gently around her neck before pulling back. Her unfocused gaze told him she was falling effortlessly into his thrall. His mating scent was growing ever stronger and affecting this small human more profoundly than any of his kind. Something about knowing that pleased him greatly.

She shoved him down her body, seeming needy and hot. He stopped to nuzzle her soft rounded breasts. They were warm and seemed to hug him back. Draconian queens barely had breasts, likely because they did not nurse their own young like some species. It suddenly occurred to him that if human queens had breasts then that meant they gave birth to their own young. His hand instinctively moved down to cup her flat stomach. "I wish to have my young here."

Wrapping her legs around him, she moved her open mouth over his neck. Her hand slid down to his hip, covering the place where he could carry their spawn. Luckily, his kind only carried for a few short weeks before the eggs were ready to be incubated in a unit. He suspected his queen would spend most of her time in the hatchery watching them grow.

When his tongue rasped over the delicate pink tip of her breast, she moaned. Eager to please, he moved back and forth between the two, licking, sucking and teasing it with his tongue until she rocking against him in a fashion that led him to believe there was something interesting between her beautiful legs that needed attention.

Pulling her legs apart, he moved down. Her queenly scent was strong enough to make his mouth water. The need to taste her felt like a punch to the gut. Rushing probably more than he should, he moved down to explore. Her folds were in keeping with her general skin tone, perhaps pinker than her lips, but lovely none the less. Looking up, he saw that she was propped up on one elbow watching him intently. Her bottom lip was dented by her teeth and she seemed more beautiful that he remembered.

One hand came down to grasp his horn and she stroked it. Pleasure surged right down his spinal cord, making his dick throb. He reached down to give it rough stroke or two. Her other hand came around and suddenly she was stroking both of his tender horns.

Leaning over, he ran his tongue over her trembling flesh. Knowing she was not only enjoying his touch but eager to ensure he experienced pleasure as well flipped all the right switches for Mathadar.

Every Draconian male was given instruction on basic health issues, including proper intercourse with a queen. All he had to do was adapt the approach for a human queen. There were some differences, most importantly her size. Careful to keep his teeth away, he explored her body in ways he'd never dreamed to do with a queen.

Bumping into a tiny nub turned out to be her hot spot. The more he teased it, the louder she got. Something about the cause and effect of licking her and feeling her squirm and moan made him want her writhing on his cock.

He could tell the moment she came, because her trembling legs tightened against him and nectar squirted in a gush against his tongue. Carefully moving up, he wanted all that wetness covering his cock. "Do you wish all of me, my queen?"

Her eyes opened and her happy gaze warmed his soul. "I do if you want to give it to me." Glancing down, her mouth fell open. "It'll fit. I promise."

That was the moment he began to doubt he would. Being so eager to touch and taste a queen for the first time, he'd forgotten to do those calculations. Compared to one of his own queens, he was appropriately sized. Unfortunately, the opening for human queens seemed rather small to Mathadar. This realization felt like being doused with cold liquid. No honorable male wished to take his pleasure at the expense of a queen. He began to kneel again, forcing himself to be content with pleasuring her with his tongue. That alone was a treat he never expected to enjoy.

His new queen was having none of that, for she grasped his hand and pulled him down beside her on the sleeping platform. Perhaps she was sated for now and wished to be held. Though breathless, his queen hauled herself up and threw one leg over his hips.

"What do you do, my queen?" The queen on top is the traditional mating position for Draconians and it seems like an impossible task she is attempting.

Smiling down at him, Mathadar admired how her unruly hair streamed down her shoulders, clinging to the sheen of sweat covering her body. Her beautiful body was blushing pink from the orgasm. Draconian queens do not change color that way. He found it extremely arousing.

~ Cassandra ~

This man is going to be the death of me. My oversensitive clit is still tingling from the long drawn out orgasm he gave me with that wicked tongue of his. Every single hardship I ever endured was worth it to find Mathadar. He's so worldly about fighting, commanding a ship full of battled hardened warriors and even great about backing me up when the breeders tried to horn in our fun. Yet, when it comes to taking his clothes off, he's about as innocent as they come.

"What do you think I'm doing, hot stuff?"

His eyes got big and his tail snaked around to slip between her legs. She grabbed it with one hand and pulled it back out again. The slightly devious look on his face says it's taboo. "You're a very naughty warrior tonight."

"I wish to experience everything in one night, in case you send me away on the morrow."

"It's called 'tomorrow' and you don't need to worry about that. We've got our whole lives to explore each other's bodies."

Her hands smoothed over his torso, lingering on his lower abdomen. "You don't have a navel because you're hatched, right?"

His chin came up slightly. "Only weak creatures have such frailties. Draconian warriors have plating under our skin to protect us from damage. I cannot imagine having a hole in my stomach. It would make me vulnerable."

"Do you think I'm weak because I have a belly button?"

$\sim$ Mathadar $\sim$

Mathadar lowered his hand to touch the area they were discussing. "I believe it is decorative on one such as you, my queen. Your soft skin is a pleasure to touch. You have no need of hard plating to cover your vulnerable spots, for you have me to protect you."

"Aww, you say the sweetest things."

Grasping her around the waist, he pulled her over his thick cock, grinding himself into her tender flesh. "I speak only the truth. I would gladly give my life to protect you."

She moaned, rubbing herself against him as well. A suspicion was growing in his mind that they were of the same mind about breeding. It would take so little for his queen to mount him at this point. Feeling emboldened by her response, he lifted her slightly. When she reached down to position his cock, he quickly maneuvered her where she needed to be.

Placing both palms on his chest, she began to sink slowly down. Mathadar wasn't sure if it was considered polite behavior by her people, but he wished to see them joining. Staring down at her struggling to take his massive member provoked even more of mating scent to release.

Mathadar realized it was probably getting into the ventilation system. The other warriors would know he'd been bred and would be irritated by the offensive odor. He worried that it might draw the other queens to him, for queens were drawn to a male's mating scent. All he could think about was rolling over and claiming her in one hard thrust. Naturally, he forced himself to remain still beneath her because dominating a queen that way was taboo.

When she finally took the last of him, her quivering body stilled. He glanced up to find a look of pure female pride on her face. Shock rippled through his mind that she would feel pride at such an accomplishment. His queen deserved all the pleasure he could give.

He brought up his wings to cushion her back and one hand drifted down to tease at the tiny bud he'd discovered earlier. This time she didn't protest; instead she started to move up and down his cock, sliding out a little more with each movement of her hips.

He watched as she got lost pleasuring herself on his cock. Pert breasts bounced in his face and he got lost in the sheer pleasure of seeing, hearing and feeling her eager body moving against his.

Mathadar wished nothing more than to protect and pleasure his queen, keeping her tucked carefully under his wings for all time. Learning that he was to be her one and only male made the whole situation seem like some kind of fantastic dream.

Having her moving over him reminded him of the inappropriate thoughts he had when he saw her bound in the marketplace. Seeing her trussed up with her hands above her head and her beautiful breasts on display as she struggled to free herself had made him hard. Now his wildest dream had come true and provoked a deep level of possessiveness that bordered on dangerous. Mathadar knew he'd kill to keep her all to himself, and that wasn't the Draconian way.

Being called her Takadon was everything he ever wanted. Forcing himself to hold back until she came took all his discipline as a warrior. When her movements became jerky, he worried that he was simply too much for her. She collapsed on his chest, whispering, "Roll us. I want to be on the bottom. It's your turn to do the heavy lifting again."

Mathadar found himself complying with that request before he could fully process the implications of what she was asking. Covering his mate was another wild perverse fantasy he only recently had been sexually advanced enough to think up.

He thrust gently, causing her frustrated voice to sound off. "Harder, my Takadon. I won't break."

Silken legs came up around his waist, jerking him forward roughly. Feeling her limbs bumping against his wing base tipped him over the edge, ripping away what little self-control he'd managed to hang onto. He thrust into her soft, warm body with a quickening pace, careful not to use his full strength against her. It seemed the rougher he was, the more she verbalized her pleasure.

Suddenly, her body seized and she bowed slightly off the sleeping platform. It felt like nothing Mathadar could have ever imagined. The pleasure was so extreme it bordered on pain. He barely moved and it was enough to have him emptying inside her in long hard spasms that made him see dark spots in his vision. He'd never heard of a male dying from pleasure, but in that moment it almost felt possible.

Stilling inside her, he realized the mixture of his mating scent and her pheromones hung heavy in the air. His queen was ripe for the taking and since human queens gave birth as well, chances were good they were now both with child. His hand drifted down to her stomach. His child was likely growing there. As if intuiting his thoughts again, her hand dropped down to where even now he could feel parthenogenesis taking place.

Looking down at her still-blushing body, he murmured, "I regret only that my young will not have your lovely hair."

She struggled to catch her breath. "I'd love our sons to look just like their father."

They both knew that a Draconian male's reproductive system produced almost a carbon copy of the sire. It was one of the reasons they weren't seen as individuals. He remembered how she loved holding the young in the hatchery. She would be a good queen mother to their young. Mathadar felt that all the way down to his soul.

Forcing himself to pull out, he allowed her to curl up to his side and brought both wings up to shelter her.

"That was nothing short of amazing."

"Shall I assume that you are keeping me, my queen?"

Yawning, she cuddled closer. "You should assume that you're never getting rid of me. I want you and only you at my side and in my bed forever."

Nuzzling his face in her hair, he sighed. "Though my mating scent is waning even as we speak, forever is an acceptable length of time for me as well. I hope you will be true to your word about being satisfied with less."

Tilting her head up, she kissed his chin. "Humans prefer quality over quantity, handsome."

"You think me to be a quality male?"

"You're the best at everything. Nobody understands me like you do. Plus I'm a huge fan of your lovemaking skills."

"I believe you love the revidian almost as much as my cock."

"The revidian? What the heck is that?"

"The revidian is when I have my mouth on your tender flesh." Her face became pink again and Mathadar couldn't resist teasing her. "It is when my tongue dances between your delicate folds, teasing the tiny bead until you squirm and try to close your legs."

"You've got a dirty mouth for such a restrained guy."

"I am not used to speaking plainly to a queen. You allow me privileges no Draconian male has known in many long centuries."

Smiling up at him, she asked, "What are we going to do when I revidian you?"

"I do not believe even the most perverse queens do this for their males."

"There's that word again. I'm not sure I like every out-of-the-ordinary thing we do being called perverse."

"I apologize, my queen. I intended no insult."

"Just so you know, nothing is forbidden between a male and a female on my home world. As long as both are agreeable and no one gets hurt, the sky's the limit."

Turning slightly, Mathadar found he was extremely interested in the sexual mores of humans. "What if I wished the reverse-revidian and you wished to bestow such a gift, would it be permitted?"

"We do that all the time on Earth."

Mathadar's cock hardened immediately. "I have many perverse ideas that come into my head. Therefore, I do not think you will wish to open the door in such a welcoming manner, my queen."

She turned slightly as well until they were facing each other.

"What other sexy ideas do you have rolling around in that head of yours, handsome?"

Picking through the thoughts in his head, Mathadar came up with a particularly deviant thought. "I wish to mark you with seed and have you wear my scent all day, so the breeders and other warriors know you are mine."

"I thought you *were* mine. Isn't that the way things work in your world?"

Nodding, he quickly explained, "That is what makes my wish such a perversion."

"I see. I have a sexy fantasy similar to that."

Hauling in a deep breath, he encouraged her to voice it. "Tell me now, my queen, how I may best serve you."

"I had a dream once. You came to my quarters while I was sleeping, ripped all my clothing off, and made me touch myself while you watched."

It felt like every cell in his body flared to life all at the same time. "You truly wish this?"

"Oh, I'm not done yet. In my dream, you really got off on seeing me touching myself, so you stroked yourself and came on my breasts. When you rubbed it in with those big rough hands, it was so hot I came immediately."

His chest swelled with a multitude of emotions, so many he couldn't name them all if he wanted to. His nostrils flared and he stated flatly, "I will do this and you will wear my scent. Are we agreed?"

Moving close, she pressed her body to his. "Sure thing, handsome. We'll do that real soon."

Mathadar wrapped his tail around her slim waist and inhaled their mingled scents. This small queen made his life worth living. He only wished that if any of his brothers survived, they somehow had the good fortune of finding a way out of the clutches of the Draconian queens, as Mathadar had.

18 TWISTED ETHICS

CASSANDRA

Cassandra woke when strong arms lifted her from the bed and carried her to the cleansing unit. The big broad chest was a virtual wall of muscles. Stretching her arms slightly, she hauled in a lungful of air. "Good morning, my Takadon."

His crisp reply caught her off-guard. "It is good afternoon, my queen. We slept the morning away." Something about his voice sounded like gentle chiding.

"Haven't you ever slept in?"

"Never. It is forbidden for warriors to waste precious time sleeping when there is work to be done."

"I think your queen will be understanding just this once. Having sex multiple times a night can be tiring."

"My queen has an unquenchable thirst for my cock. She woke me over and over again throughout the night to ride me with abandon."

Cassandra couldn't help the stunned expression on her face. "Are you sure all the sex didn't addle your brain? According to my recollection it was you who couldn't get enough of your queen, not vice versa."

"There must have been a communication breakdown last night, for that is not my recollection of the events."

"Communication breakdown? That's what you want to call it, is it? Well, I call it mutual lust."

His big body shook again with laughter. Happiness zinged through her chest. Seeing her normally reserved commander joking around was nothing short of amazing.

Starting the mister with one hand, he dumped her feet-first into the cleansing unit before stepping in behind her. "Wow, you've got miles and miles of muscles there, Math. No clothing is a really good look for you."

Turning to look over his shoulder, he looked at her mouth. "You should guard your mouth, my queen."

"What the hell does that even mean?" Cassandra sputtered.

"I knew you chose me because you made the mating gesture to me. I think you make it to other males by mistake. I have even seen you make the mating gesture to females. It must be confusing for them."

"Again, what in the 'verse are you talking about?"

"Among my people when a female wishes to attract the attention of a male, she shows him her best feature, her sharp teeth. That is how the male knows he is chosen."

"Wait a doggone minute. Smiling is considered a mating gesture among your people?"

Nodding, he responded sincerely, "It is, but only if the queen shows her teeth."

Thinking over his words, she now had an explanation for the extremely toothy grin he gave her in return the first time she smiled at him. At the time it seemed bizarrely forced and like he intended on displaying every single tooth in his head. "Since all your queens have sharp teeth, I suppose that makes sense. I guess it's also why they never reverse-revidian anyone."

"Not all males have plating on their cocks. The few who do have such plating well know it is not sufficient to protect them from a malicious queen. Their teeth are razor-sharp."

Just when Cassandra thought there was nothing he could do to shock her, he comes out with something else. Trying to keep from thinking of a huge Draconian using her vicious teeth on a male, she tried to lighten things up. "Just so you know, I'm going to reverse-revidian you the very first chance I get. What do you think of that?"

Snorting a laugh, his wings jerked. "Your blunt little teeth will pose no threat to my cock."

Reaching out to grab his cock, she rubbed cleansing foam over it in long slow strokes before allowing the mister to wash it away. Dropping to her knees, she gave him another long, languid stroke. His arms crashed into the wall and he stumbled backward, his wings unfurling to the point that they took up the entire rear of the mister.

"My queen ...you should not." Snapping his mouth closed, he stared down at her with a strange mixture of absolute shock and fascination.

For a brief moment, she thought that maybe he was honestly transgressed. The moment he pushed his hips closer to her face she knew he wanted what she was offering, he just didn't think he should. She reached out for his hand. He reluctantly tangled his fingers in her hair. "Tell me what you want, gorgeous. Say the words."

His nostrils flared in that sexy way that told her he was on the edge again. "You wish to hear more perversions from my lips?"

"Yes. I want to taste you."

His fingers gripped her hair tighter. It stung, but

nothing was going to stop her from pleasuring her sexy man the way he deserved, the way he pleasured her a half dozen times last night. When he spoke his voice was deep and rough. "Suck my cock. I wish to feel your delicate human tongue against my skin."

Leaning over, she kissed the tip and swirled her tongue around. His blue skin was a slightly deeper color where it counted. He was one of the warriors with plating on his cock. It ran down the underside of his rod, growing smaller toward the tip. Fat rings bulged out from around it and when she touched them, they felt more like the kind of cartilage found at the top of her own ear. She vaguely remembered how those rings felt when he pounded into her last night. Leaning over again, she was about to do just like he asked and suck him dry.

That's when the ship rocked underneath them. His smoking-hot expression fell away in a heartbeat, replaced by one of concern. "We are under attack, my queen. Come, we must hurry."

"I'm putting my money on your old queen coming to reclaim her warriors."

Jumping out of the cleansing unit, he held out one hand for her to take. He tugged her gently up from her knees and they ran to get dressed.

"I believe you are correct. Heinka may be addicted to Tarken, but she is tenacious. Since her primary target was Queen Teladora, I fear Heinka has found and dispatched the young queen if she has come for us."

Pulling the skintight space suits over damp skin was a bitch, but they managed in record time.

"I'm not counting Tela out quite yet. She's smart and savvy. Maybe she outsmarted your old queen and slipped away." They headed for the bridge at a flat-out run. "It might not be Heinka at all. Maybe it's another queen or even the aquatics looking for some payback."

"It matters not, for I plan to kill whoever dared to interrupt my queen when she was performing critically important queenly duties."

She couldn't help but laugh. "You're hilarious, even in a crisis. I really like that in a man."

"This is the first time I've been permitted to have a sense of humor. I find it is very much to my liking."

Stumbling onto the bridge, breathless and worried, she saw it was Heinka after all. Her face lit up the display screen. If it was at all possible, she looked even worse than she did the last time they spoke.

Cassandra stepped forward. "You're not looking so good, Heinka. Sure you want to go round for round with me?"

"You will release Queen Rovanda immediately."

"I'm afraid that I can't do that. She's down for the count."

"If you have harmed her I will draw out your pain when I kill you."

"Now, let's not get ahead of ourselves."

"Speak sense, humon."

Seeing how irritated Heinka was trying to understand human dialect and idioms, Cassandra saw a rather petty way to keep her unbalanced. "I mean to say that you're putting the cart before the horse."

Waving one hand through the air, she bit back, "Enough, humon, I have no time for your craven games. If you turn my queen mother over unharmed, I will make your death short and painless."

Shaking her head at the other woman's lack of negotiation skills, Cassandra shrugged. 'That might not be as much of an incentive to play nice as you think."

"You have no other option. Surrender."

"Or what? Fire on our ship and risk killing the person you're trying to rescue? I'm betting that first round was more like a warning shot across the bow, so to speak."

Heinka's facial expression turned murderous. Her mouth opened and then closed again.

"Rovanda's your mother? I guess that's why she attacked us out of the clear blue sky. Your mother was cleaning up your mess and got herself neutralized."

"Does she yet live? What did you do to her?"

"I didn't do a thing. Her primary breeder brought her down with one of her own personal weapons."

Heinka's mouth fell open. "Pern turned on my mother? He would never do such a thing. I do not believe him capable..." She closed her mouth without finishing the sentence.

"I guess he had some grievances about the way she reaped his young or something along those lines."

"They were her own young. He was simply the breeder. We reap to ensure only the strong survive. It is for the good of all Draconians that we do not allow inferior males to join the ranks. They would weaken ...."

"I'm gonna have to call bullshit on that whole train of thought. Reaping is a really shitty thing to do."

"It's been our way for thousands of years."

"I'm not going to argue with you about that. Your mother lives. We have her in stasis."

"I will tear your ship apart if you do not return her to me at once."

"That's not how this is going to go down. You're going to surrender your ship to me if you wish your mother to live."

"I'm not weak. Surrender will enable you to kill us both at your leisure."

"The thing you're not getting is, I don't give a rat's ass if you and your mother live or die. I understand that Draconian queens challenge each other for power. It's a matter of honor. Humans simply don't care about stuff like that. I'd be happy to put you both down on some abandoned planet with a distress beacon. You have to decide which you value more, your honor or your mother's life."

"Human queens are cowards with no sense of honor."

"It's real cute how you actually think I give a crap what you think. Time to make a decision, Heinka. What's it going to be, your pride or your mother's life?"

"Come and face me in single combat, humon."

"I could do that, but once I defeat you, that offer of getting dropped off somewhere nice is no longer going to be on the table. Think it over. I'll give you a few moments to yourself."

Turning to Mathadar's stoic face, Cassandra asked, "How is it we didn't know Rovanda was Heinka's mother? That would have been handy information to have."

Mathadar dipped his head in a gesture of respect. "I do not believe Rovanda is Heinka's mother. My memory is that she was spawned on the other side of the great divide."

"Perhaps there is connection between the parasites, rather than the hosts."

"That seems more likely, my queen. Since such things were kept from us, I have no idea how to verify such a suspicion."

Thinking it over for a minute, Cassandra rubbed her temple to soothe the vein throbbing there. "Nor do I. Have Rovanda removed from the medical unit and placed into an escape pod." She gestured to the navigator. "Target a nearby planet for the drop. I prefer it to be clear of sentient life."

"Yes, my queen."

Cassandra worried over her decision to abandon the queen rather than kill her. "I don't want them preying on primitive beings who've never been in contact with aliens."

"I found a world three parsecs from our current location," the navigator said. "It's a small planet with breathable atmosphere, a brutally cold but survivable atmosphere, and no evolved species."

"That'll do just fine." Turning back to Mathadar, she asked anxiously, "If we put a distress beacon in the escape pod will any of your people respond?"

"I believe they will respond but not in the kind way you are hoping. Failed queens are dealt with harshly by their peers. I believe they will be found and executed."

"What are their chances of surviving on the planet long-term if we don't leave a distress beacon?"

Mathadar leaned over to scroll through information on a computer console. "The planet in question has animal and plant life in addition to an abundance of water. There is a stable dynamic core in place." Scrolling some more, he added, "Our scans indicate it is the correct distance from its sun and conditions are favorable for seasonal changes. It also has a large enough moon to stabilize any axis wobble."

"Are you saying they could survive long-term there?"

"Assuming they do not eventually turn on each other."

Running her hand over her face, Cassandra thought it over a minute. "We'll put a distress beacon in the pod, along with emergency provisions, but don't activate the beacon. Let the two of them decide their own destiny."

Mathadar nodded his agreement. "That is a wise and compassionate course of action, my queen."

Turning to the communications officer, Cassandra gestured to the huge screen with one hand. "Open the communications channel to Heinka again. Let's get this over with before we draw the notice of another queen."

Moments later the Draconian queen's face came up on the view screen.

Cassandra wasted no time getting to the point. "Time's up, Queen Heinka. What's your decision?"

"I will agree to a temporary ceasefire."

"There's only one offer on the table. Either your surrender or else."

"I will agree to voluntarily go down to the planet in a shuttle, but only if our males accompany us. We are queens and deserve to be served."

Cassandra was growing weary of arguing with the stubborn being. Stepping forward, she raised her voice a notch. "You're both nothing but hosts to a parasitic organism. Though everyone may be fooled by your Draconian body, I know who's in control. You infested them both when they were vulnerable teens."

"The words you so carelessly speak mean death for every warrior listening. They will not be allowed to live to repeat your lies."

"What lies? We discovered all your secrets by scanning Rovanda. We had to adapt our machinery, but it showed how your kind reproduce, taking over the host's brain and other organs. We couldn't separate host from parasite even if we wanted to at this point. You're too deeply enmeshed."

"It matters not. Draconians were a primitive species until they joined with us."

Cassandra was shocked the parasite was no longer even denying she was living off the host. "I'm growing annoyed with this back and forth."

"Let us at least take our breeders."

"If you think for a second I'm going to leave males behind for the two of you to control and abuse, you better think again. That will never happen."

"You have no right to dictate terms, humon."

Ignoring her discontent, Cassandra added, "Also know that we've scanned your ship. I know the exact number of breeders, warriors, and young you have on board. We're going to scan every inch of your ship before I send you down to the planet. If you kill or harm anyone, I'm going to revisit that pain on you three times over."

"This is an attack on my kind that will not go unanswered. No matter how far you travel, we will find you. It matters not how clever you are, how hard you fight, or how many warriors you sacrifice in battle. You will be caught and brought to justice."

"Draconian queens have a sick and twisted sense of ethics in my opinion."

19 DOUBLE-CROSSED

MATHADAR

His new queen was living proof that queens were born to rule. Never had he seen a Draconian queen back down the way Heinka did this day. It was clear that Rovanda meant something to the woman, but as far as they could tell the parasites didn't seem to spawn the way Draconians and humans did. They came from larvae in the pool. It was almost like there were a finite number of them and they simply resided in the pool until they entered a Draconian queen and ascended. They seemed to colonize the host's body. Then again, that didn't make sense either. Even the parasites had to come from somewhere.

Suddenly, a dark thought clawed forward from the back of his mind, making his blood run cold.

A delicate hand landed on his arm. "Mathadar, what's wrong? You look like you've seen a ghost."

Unsure what the last phrase meant, Mathadar knew his queen wanted to know his thoughts. "I've been thinking on how the parasites reproduce."

"I've wondered that myself. Do you think they

somehow reproduce in the queen's body and she goes back to spawn in the waters?"

"I do not."

"What are you thinking?"

Looking around the bridge, he saw every set of eyes were trained upon him. "I do not wish to frighten you, my queen. However, I wish you to know of our myths in order that you might make the most correct decision in our time of need."

Feeling anxiety twist in her gut, Cassandra muttered, "I get the feeling I'm not going to like this particular story."

Stepping forward, he took her hands in his. "The elders in my line told of the time before writing. Many Draconian clades have special powers such as being able to see the future or the ability to see complex patterns that others miss. Some are talented at healing or navigate instinctually. My clade is known as the keeper of myths, for we have an uncanny ability to remember complex stories in great detail. If my line can be accused of having a special ability, this would be it."

Forcing herself to calm down, she pulled herself together. "Tell me what you know, my Takadon. Your information may save lives and help us find a way through this mess."

His voice dropped slightly as he began to speak. "The elders once told stories of a creature, hunted and despised by all." Glancing around, his hands tightened around hers. "You must first know that to speak of such things is considered heresy and is punishable by death."

Frowning up at him, she shot back, "I have a quick question. Is there any mistake a warrior can make that's not punishable by death? I'm only asking because every single thing you guys do wrong seems to come with a death penalty."

Swallowing thickly, Mathadar's eyes slid away for a brief moment before returning to land on her. "You are not far from wrong about that, my sweet queen."

"Just tell me what you want me to know. I promise everything will be okay."

Nodding, he began his tale. "Our elders told a story of a creature who was thrown down to our planet by the gods. It was said the animal was vicious and filled with deceit. This creature's mating song was so powerful no male could resist her. She wreaked unimaginable damage on many worlds before finally being tracked down, captured, and imprisoned on a planet with beings not affected by her song. It is said that our ancient ancestors would not recognize her if we were staring her in the face, because she was as different to us as night is to the day."

"I'm not understanding, my Takadon."

Sighing, he closed his eyes for a moment as if to remember. "I was told as a small spawn that the creature landed in our oceans and took up residence in the deepest, darkest spot, hidden where no one would ever find her. It is the reason our people do not swim in the salty waters of our home world. We have no wish to be dragged down into the murky depths by such an aquatic."

"Are you saying this sea creature is longed lived and is still hiding there to this day?"

"No, my queen. I'm saying she is not in our oceans at all, but rather in the waters of the cave of ascension. Think about it for a moment. These creatures do not seem to mature and spawn like other beings. That can only mean one thing. Their queen resides in the waters in the cave."

"That doesn't make sense. Tela told me she walked

through the waters and though it covered her head, it was not deep like an ocean."

"I believe she trod on the creature itself rather than the ground."

Horror doubled and then tripled in Cassandra's mind. "If what you say is true, Draconians have been sending their young girls right into heart of the darkness for thousands of years."

"I worry that our queens have mingled with the parasites for so long they have accepted their fate. Perhaps they even embrace the parasites as a way to gain intelligence and power over not only their males but all the species in this sector of space."

Staring up the battle-hardened warrior, Cassandra shook her head. "I'm not buying that. If the queens wanted to embrace the parasites in some type of symbiotic relationship, the whole thing wouldn't have been kept top secret for thousands of years. They're hiding it from the young queens and have taken over this sector of space in an effort to make sure no one captures that creature again."

"It is likely you speak the truth, my queen." Mathadar's voice was filled with a lifetime of grief and it just about broke Cassandra's heart.

"I'd give just about anything to destroy that creature once and for all. Think about it. If it can no longer breed, then after a few generations the parasites would die out."

"You speak dangerous words, my queen, words that would have every queen in the sector seeking your blood."

Folding her arms over her chest, Cassandra stepped back. "For the first time in my life I'm thinking that some things are worth dying for, and killing that queen might be one of them."

"Where you go, I will follow. As your Takadon, I will do all in my power to keep you safe."

"Let's dispense with Rovanda and Heinka first. She followed us as we knew she would, so putting her on the planet should prove to be no problem if she keeps her word about surrendering. It is unlikely she will go without a fight or using some form of treachery.

"We'll have to be alert and keep our eyes open for any trickery on her part. Once we've dealt with the two of them, we'll have two ships and almost two thousand warriors at our disposal. We'll meet up with Tela and get her take on the whole situation."

"If Tela managed to secured her training ship without sacrificing the reptilian vessel, we will have four ships and close to twenty-five hundred warriors. It is still a small number in relation to the number of queens who will come for us, but we can create battle plans to take advantage of our strengths and compensate for our weaknesses," Math-adar said.

When Heinka's face lit up the screen, she was looking pretty bad. Sweat made her skin look wet and her horns and tail were hanging limply. "Ready to fight for what you want or are you still intent on stealing all that I have like a thief crouching in the darkness, humon?"

"We're not going over that again. I want you in an escape pod immediately."

"The deal was I go in a shuttle."

Gritting her teeth, Cassandra gave approval for shuttle transport. "Fine. Go in a shuttle, but do it now before I change my mind. We'll be scanning you the entire time. I don't want any shenanigans. If you try anything at all, we'll blast you out of the sky and Rovanda will pay for your mistake."

"Do not touch Rovanda. She is the only queen in the fleet that I would sacrifice myself for."

"I know she's not your mother. If you tell me why she's so special, I'll be sure to handle her with special care. There won't be a single mark on her precious body."

The other queen stared at her for a long hard moment before answering. "Though you may not see it, Vithacans are honorable creatures. We have a hierarchy where the oldest and most intelligent are respected. Rovanda is one of our elders, though the body of her host is not. She was my mentor, teaching me all that I know about the 'verse."

Suddenly, Cassandra was angry. "I'll just bet she did. Did she walk you through the joy of tormenting your first warrior? Perhaps she helped you learn how to blow up planets and harvest the precious metals hidden deep in the core? Someone had to teach you the basics of reaping your own young. Was it Rovanda?"

The woman's expression closed down and her voice became tight. "Draconians are but the meat upon which we feed. Do you feel sorry for the plant and animal matter that comprise your meals?"

"I don't understand."

"Vithacans are soul-suckers," Mathadar whispered. "They feed off the emotions of sentient beings. We thought they were of myth."

Cassandra gasped. "I can't believe you put a name to your kind."

"It matters not. The other queens will hunt you down before you can make it out of the Exion. They will kill you and every male who heard us speak. There is nowhere you can go that will be safe from our wrath."

Cassandra felt sick to her stomach. "You're a nasty piece of work. I hope you know that, Heinka."

Heinka's voice rang out again. "We did not choose to be as we are. The universe has a natural order. Is it our fault that we are higher on the food chain than both Draconians and humons?"

Having had enough of the parasite's enlightenment to last a lifetime, Cassandra spat our orders. "Get in your shuttle alone. Pack it with all the luxuries you like, but do it now."

"You leave me no choice, humon."

"We'll be watching to make sure you leave alone. Once you hit the ground, we'll send Rovanda's escape pod down. You'll have to take her out of stasis."

When the screen went blank, Cassandra spun around to face her crew. "I want to disable communications and weapons on that shuttle once it lands."

"We have weapons that can simply make all the shuttle's power systems inoperable. Targeting the shuttle would not be difficult once it is on the ground."

"Do it. Also pull the distress beacon from Rovanda's pod. I don't want them out torturing and reaping again in this lifetime."

Mathadar dipped his head slightly. "It will be according to your commands, my queen."

Cassandra paced while her crew scurried around getting in place around the planet, making final adjustments to Rovanda's pod and monitoring Heinka's ship. It took close to fifty microns for the loading bay doors on Heinka's ship to open. They watched on the screen as her shuttle flew out, straight for the designated planet.

"Scan it thoroughly. Make sure she didn't bring any of her breeders with her."

"She skirted around your orders by bringing seven unhatched spawn."

"Target her engines and weapons. I want her shuttle disabled and then use a grappling hook to tow her into our loading bay."

"You mean to challenge her over the eggs?"

"Hell yes. Draconian queens don't give a shit about their young. She's just going to raise them to be slaves and I'm not having it."

Mathadar's eyes grew warm and approving. "Rescuing the little unhatched spawn will earn you the endless gratitude of her breeders."

"I'm not interested in breeders, my Takadon. One big sexy warrior is enough for me."

The hastily spoken teasing was enough to pull the other crewmembers out of their morose mood. Everyone seemed to breathe a little easier and wings lifted a little higher, but none as high as her commander's.

"Weapons away, Queen Cassandra. We're targeting her primary weapons first," Dar said from one of the consoles.

They watched white star-shaped light collide with a round hub on the top of the shuttle. Several smaller bursts hit other areas of the shuttle, causing it rock precariously. "Weapons are down. We're now targeting her ..."

Before he could finish, Heinka's furious face filled the view screen. "I followed your rules and yet you fire on my shuttle. What kind of trickery is this?"

For lack of better options, Cassandra tore a page from the Draconian queen's handbook and lied her ass off. "I didn't get to them in time to stop their attack, for I was speaking with Rovanda. She has awoken and commands to speak with us. I believe our goals may not mutually exclusive."

Heinka straightened. "Rovanda is wise."

"I agree. She told me many things of which I had no knowledge. I see things differently now."

Letting out a deep sigh, she nodded slightly with sweat still dripping down her entire body. "I am not surprised that she could get you to see reason."

"Dock with our ship and I will escort you to her chamber."

Heinka's chin lifted. "I will be armed, so do not think me weak."

"I would never think you weak. In fact I have a gift of Tarken for you as an offering of peace between us."

Relief flooded her face. "Then let there be temporary peace between us."

The screen went blank again and Cassandra murmured under her breath, "You're not weak, just stupid."

Mathadar's anxious voice voiced his concern. "What is your plan, my queen? Heinka is not to be trifled with. Though she seems weakened by her lack of the Tarken, I believe she is even more dangerous. Prolonged use of the drug causes a kind of madness you have likely never seen. Having both queens on our ship is a danger beyond our ability to manage."

"I say we simply give her what she most desires. Some of your original team secured a small quantity of the drug. We will gift her with the Tarken, but I wish it to be mixed with a strong sedative, much like the one Pern used to drug Rovanda."

"This may work if she does not taste the drug."

"Have our healers place it in a nasal inhaler. My people use them to introduce medications into the soft tissues of the lungs. It is absorbed quicker into the bloodstream. Tell them to hurry. We don't have much time."

"I will see it done, my queen." Mathadar brought his

communications unit to his lips and spoke into it as Cassandra began to pace once more.

Mathadar's hand landed on her shoulder and she froze. He pulled her back and wrapped both arms around her small body. "Do not worry, my queen. You have made plans inside of plans and we will not fail you. Come. Heinka's shuttle is docking."

"Guard your eyes, my Takadon. She will be looking for any excuse to get her claws into you. I need her to believe our farce long enough for her to ingest the Tarken."

"I will avoid her gaze. No matter what happens, stay focused on the plan. If it comes to an all-out brawl, she will kill as many as she can, beginning with you."

"Let's not give her a chance to lose her shit. I'll do the meet and greet, act all submissive, and give her the Tarken. Once she's down, we put her in an escape pod and down to the planet."

"We will see to the eggs when she hits the ground."

Cassandra nodded. Something about this situation felt like a catastrophe in the making. It felt like Heinka was giving in a bit too easily. Then again, she seemed earnest about her belief that Rovanda could sway any woman's mind to her way of thinking. Mathadar was correct about how dangerous it was to have them both on board. Try as she might, Cassandra just couldn't figure out what was nagging at the back of her mind. It felt like they wanted something from her that she probably wasn't going to want to give.

They were met at the entrance to the loading bay by a team of healers. One stepped forward with a case containing two long sleek metal objects. She lifted one from the case, realizing it had a lid fitting almost seamlessly about a fourth of the way down one end. A quick yank later and she saw the end had a hole that would just about fit a Draconian queen's nasal cavity.

One of the healers spoke. "We've blended the Tarken with a strong sedative that should be effective with just one dose. We believe she will be suspicious of such an unusual gift. Do not be surprised if she asks you to use it first."

"I'm guessing a dose calibrated to knock out a Draconian queen might put me down for good."

The other healer stepped forward with a hypo-spray. "We've mixed an inoculation that should protect you from both the Tarken and the sedative."

"I do not like the word 'should,'" Mathadar said. "It does not sound like you are certain this mixture will be effective."

Closing the unit, she placed it back into its case. "I'll take my chances. Give it to me now. She's docking and will be expecting us."

Mathadar grabbed the healer's hand in midair as he brought the hypo-spray to her neck. "This is too risky, my queen. Please reconsider your decision."

Peeling her Takadon's fingers from the other man's, she smoothed a hand down his chest. "There are no guarantees in life. If I go down, take Ravonda's weapon from my holster and fight down to the last warrior. Protect the hatchery and get them the hell off this ship. If I don't recover, you will choose another queen, perhaps Aiko Hara. I want you to rendezvous with Tela and make those aquatics in our Guared tell you where Earth is and get the hell out of this sector of space. Lead all your males to freedom in the Naxis and live a long happy life."

Cupping her chin, he tilted her head up to look into her eyes. "You are my life. Without you there will be no happiness."

"You gotta stop, my Takadon. Let them give me the inoculation. I trust you to follow my orders."

Jerking his head to one side, he sucked in a shuddering breath. "Do it before I change my mind."

A moment later Cassandra felt the sting of medication being pressed through the skin on her neck by the hypo-spray. When the healer's hand fell back down, she felt the same. "At least I didn't have an immediate reaction to the inoculation. Let's get this over with, my Takadon."

20 NOW OR NEVER

CASSANDRA

Stepping across the threshold into the loading bay, Cassandra caught sight of Heinka in person for the first time. The woman was barely holding it together. Still sweating and bleary-eyed, her movements seemed jerky in some ways that Rovanda's hadn't been. Having some experience with tweakers back on Earth, Cassandra well knew how unpredictable they could be.

Steeling her spine, she walked forward to meet the quickly deteriorating queen. Cassandra plastered a closed-mouthed smile on her face, mindful of Mathadar's schooling about showing teeth being a mating gesture among the Draconians. Heinka's eyes slid over her opponent's slight form and she apparently had a difficult time keeping a hint of smugness off her face.

"Welcome, Heinka."

"It's *Queen* Heinka, humon. Where is Queen Rovanda?"

"She is awaiting our arrival. I believe she is in the process of explaining to Pern just how much she didn't appreciate him turning one of her weapons against her. To be honest, things were getting a bit gruesome."

"Human queens have no stomach for blood sport then?"

Placing her hand over her stomach, Cassandra put on her best expression of revulsion. "I would have to say no, we do not. I honestly don't see how Draconian queens manage it."

"You need a symbiont. That will right that problem immediately." Glancing down Cassandra's body again, she shook her head. "You are small, have no claws, and are clearly a weak creature. What possible reason could Rovanda have for sparing your life, much less allowing us to meet as equals? It makes no sense."

"Humans fight with our minds, not our bodies," Cassandra responded cryptically, tapping the side of her temple. "In any event, my sector of space is rich with natural resources and we have an abundance of males eager to serve en-masse. She wishes me to lead her to my home world. There are too few queens to control our males. We need assistance and Rovanda intends to gather information and present it to the fleet."

"If what you say is true, they will send warships to assist you with uprisings by your males."

"This is my hope. I came here to learn how your queens control so many while being so few in number." Holding the box up, she pulled the lid back. "My people inhale our preferred substances. It is absorbed by the lungs and the effect is quicker and more pronounced. I had the Tarken placed into an inhaler for your convenience."

Heinka's eyes got big. One shaking hand came up to lovingly caress a canister. "This is too good to be true. Therefore I do not believe you, humon."

"My name's Queen Cassandra. How about if I use it first? Will that alleviate your fears?"

The other woman's head turned to pin Cassandra with angry eyes. "I do not fear. Fear is for the weak."

Dipping her head as she'd seen the warriors do to indicate agreement, she held the box out. "Then accept my generous gift before I decide to take it back."

The Draconian queen eyed her suspiciously. "We will each take one and use it at the same time," she stated flatly.

"Agreed. I've never had so much of a problem giving a simple gift before."

Lifting one from the case, Cassandra started to pull the top off the cylinder. Heinka's hand came out, plucking it from her grasp. "I will take this one. You must take the one I leave behind."

"Are all Draconian queens so bossy?"

"We are. Now let us enjoy the nectar of the gods."

Both brought the inhalers up and sprayed at the same time. Cassandra made a show of lifting her ribcage as though she'd inhaled but tried not to take in any more than necessary.

Heinka did just the opposite. She inhaled a large dose and tilted her head back slightly. "You were right. This is Tarken and it is potent!" She took in another large dose through the other nostril. Her mouth fell open and she craned her neck enough for everyone to hear her bones pop. "Yes. This is agreeable. Now take me to my mentor."

They began walking across the loading bay and Heinka stumbled. Her head shot around to look at the assembled group of warriors. She could clearly sense something was off, but she strode forward once more. Suddenly, her wings touched the floor and she careened forward, grabbing for Cassandra.

"You! What have you done to me, humon? Rovanda will have your head for this."

Mathadar wrapped his arms around Cassandra's waist and his wings flapped once and then again. Everything seemed to go fuzzy and darkness began closing in from the edges of her vision. At some point she realized that Mathadar had her in the air and they were backing away from the furious Draconian queen. Her eyelids grew heavy and the warmth of her Takadon's arms lulled her into a dream state. That's when it all slipped away.

Cassandra woke up with a jolt when it felt like someone had injected pure adrenaline into her chest. One of the healers was pulling back a hypo-spray from her neck. Her hand flew to her still-stinging flesh. Hauling in a deep breath, she stared into Mathadar's worried eyes.

"Are you well, my queen?"

"I feel like I just got hit by a runaway drone."

"Stay still, my queen. Let the healers finish looking you over."

"I think I'm okay. Whatever they revived me with was a bit of a shock."

"Apologies, Queen Cassandra. The sedative suppressed your respiratory system. We had to introduce a strong medication to counteract it. We have very limited knowledge of human queens."

"Well, you have some of us to study now. I'm sure you'll figure it out."

Mathadar assisted her in sitting up. She looked around, trying to figure out what happened. Heinka was lying on the floor with several warriors standing over her, where they were placing a stasis strip down her body.

A strong hand rubbed her back. "Take a few minutes and breathe deeply. Give yourself time to recover."

She nodded, still feeling as though she'd had the wind knocked out of her. Heinka didn't look injured as they placed her in a nearby escape pod and loaded her upright in a deployment chute. Strangely enough she seemed to be sleeping. Right before they shut the door, Cassandra rolled a stasis canister over. One of the warriors tossed it into the pod and sealed the door.

A hover board drifted by with Rovanda's stasis pod strapped on top. Cassandra came to her feet as the warriors loaded the pod into another chute. Mathadar slipped his wing behind her body and tucked her to his side.

Glancing up at his proud expression, she turned to see what had caught his eye. Several breeders were hovering around a rack of incubation units, each containing a single egg. Fascinated, Cassandra walked over to gaze at them through the glass. One looked very different from the rest. The others were like she'd always imagined dinosaur eggs would look. However, one was larger, broader, and had a different coloration. Instead of a pattern of dark green and purple, the larger egg was solid black. She brought her hand up to touch the glass. "This one's really pretty."

Mathadar shook slightly with amusement, his wings squeezing her close. "The dark one is female. All the rest are males."

Turing to Valden, she jerked her chin toward the door. "Get them into the hatchery and invite the fathers to come and stay onboard our vessel. Make them feel welcome."

"Yes, my queen. Thank you for rescuing the hatchlings."

"It was my pleasure."

Watching them wheel the incubation chambers away, she sighed. "That was too close a call. We need to gather all the kids and put them in the safest location possible."

"I agree. Shall we deploy the pods?"

Nodding, she snuggled closer to his warm body.

Mathadar spoke up. "Deploy Rovanda and then Heinka, with a one-micron delay."

Cassandra watched them deploy Rovanda's pod, and it was followed by Heinka's pod a few moments later. Something about seeing each of them slide away started a chain reaction in her brain leading to the epiphany of a lifetime. Bringing her hands to her head, she stepped from under Mathadar's wing.

"What is wrong, my queen? We have been successful beyond our wildest dreams."

Pivoting to face him, she shook with anger. "I'm making a run for the Draconian home world."

"You are going to hunt for the Vithacan queen mother, are you not?"

Nodding, she tried to speak to what was in her heart. "I know that I'm not a warrior, Mathadar. But I can't just leave her in the cave infecting generation after generation of your women. I wouldn't be able to live with myself."

"This is an impossible quest, my sweet one. Even if we could get within striking distance of the queen, we have no idea what she's like. Perhaps she is something that cannot be killed by mortal hands."

"I have to try."

"The commander is correct. You'll never make it, Cassandra." The breathless feminine voice sounded like she'd been running for miles.

Peering around Mathadar, she saw Tela step from one of the docking rings. Rushing over to her, Cassandra flung her arms around the younger Draconian queen. "I missed you, Tela."

Her female friend made a chirping sound that sounded

like laughter. "I have never been hugged by a queen before, but thank you." Shoving her back gently, Tela looked amused. "I worried about your ability to make your way in the 'verse. It pleases me to see you've not only survived but defeated two Draconian queens. I must admit to being more than a little shocked."

"I wouldn't say I defeated them exactly—more like tricked them."

"I no longer think we should fight fairly. A less-than-honorable victory is preferable to death. Congratulations, my friend."

Looking around at the multitude of males in her entourage, Cassandra saw there were two other extremely young Draconian queens. One looked to be in her early teens and the other around ten years old. "Who do you have here?"

"This is Trace, my Takadon."

A handsome oversized male stepped forward. He was topless, exposing miles of gorgeous muscles and golden skin. "I am pleased to meet the queen who rescued my Teladora." Rather than going down on one knee for a queen who was not his own, he half-bowed before slipping his wing back around Tela.

"Aren't you adorable?"

Patting his chest, Tela practically purred, "He's my perfect one."

Cassandra laughed. "I thought you had a stable of breeders."

"You are not wrong, my new human friend. Trace is my companion as well as my breeder. It is a concept I learned from you."

"Well, good luck with that."

Turning to the tween, Tela introduced her as well.

"This is Bejkatonda. She has seen twelve solars and wishes to avoid being sullied by the parasites. She comes with her sire and fourteen brothers. Her males were forced to kill their queen to free her."

Cassandra stepped forward at the same time as Bejka, meeting her halfway. "Greetings, Bejka. Welcome to our ship and to freedom if we can manage to find our way out of this sector of space. I am sorry for the loss of your queen mother."

The young girl nodded, seeming older than her stated age. "As am I, Queen Cassandra. We thank you for granting us the knowledge of the cave. If not for that I would have been taken there when my time came."

"Join us and we will talk about how to best get you free of this place."

The young queen barely dipped her head in response. Drawing her long gown together more tightly, she stuffed her small hands into the sleeves.

Tela walked Cassandra over to the one who appeared to be nine or so. "This is Nanabella. Her sire did not dispose of her when his queen demanded. Instead he hid her away in the bowels of his ship. She had never met another queen before me. Nana is too innocent to be tasked with making decisions, for she has only seen eight turns of the seasons."

Even this eight-year-old queen was tall enough to look Cassandra in the eye. Yet it was clear that she wasn't fully developed. Her horns were tiny and her tail didn't even reach her knees. She was wearing a bright purple flight suit and looked a little rough.

"Welcome, Nana," Cassandra greeted her gingerly. "It's a pleasure to meet you."

Looking from the scarred male at her side and then back

to Cassandra, she murmured, "Please do not harm my sire Gorok. He only wished to see me grow up."

"Oh honey, we're not going to touch your father. He's as welcome here as you are. We'll make sure he stays right with you, how about that?"

"Thank you, Queen Cassie. Tela told us so much about you and I can see she was telling the truth. You are small and nice."

Cassandra motioned to one of the warriors. "Maybe the nursery would be a better fit for Queen Nana. She'll have other children to play with there."

"Yes, my queen." He led them to the door and presumably to the hatchery, looking confused.

Turning back to Tela, she asked, "So you don't think I have a chance of getting close to the Draconian home world?"

"I do not. What is this creature you speak of killing? I know of no creatures on my home world worth risking your life to hunt."

"There may be a Vithacan queen mother hiding in the cave of ascension. We think she's the only one who breeds the tiny parasites that tried to colonize your body. The healers studied them and reported back to us that they don't seem to be capable of procreating in the woman's body."

"I saw no creature in the cave."

"Could she have been hiding in the waters?"

A look of horror crossed Tela's face. "When I walked into the waters, the bottom was soft. It was gross, but I convinced myself that it was simply filthy sediment that naturally sinks to the bottom of such pools."

"I'm gonna take that as a yes."

While talking they'd been walking toward the adjacent bay with Tela's entire entourage in tow. Mathadar kept to

Cassandra's back with his wing around her in an ever-protective gesture. It was clear he didn't quite trust the newcomers.

They piled into the alien version of a spacious meeting room with hovering chairs and a huge flat hovering disk that seemed to function as a table and a viewing screen. Tela's males stood along the walls, except Trace who stayed at her back. Bejka's father sat by her side and her brothers were dispersed around the room, giving them space to talk.

Tela started the conversation in earnest. "I think we should try to get to this creature, if she does indeed exist. Of course, then we will have to find an exit strategy, because the other queens will wish nothing more than to kill us in the most painful way possible."

"Yeah, I don't want to be present for that. Any ideas on how we can get close enough to the planet to land?"

"We don't have a planetary defense shield or anything like that. Our entire planet is ringed with laser cannons. The civil defense officers can blast anything out of the air and they scan for ships constantly," Tela said.

"Could we get through if we stow away on a ship that's scheduled to land?"

"Possibly, but I'm not sure who to trust at this point. Everyone knows I'm a renegade. My face has been plastered all over the coms." Tela bolted up in her chair. "Maybe I can pretend to turn myself in and beg for another shot at ascension. If they let me get close enough, I'll kill the creature."

Bejka's quiet voice interjected. "I might be able to get through. We can make up a new persona for me. If we're quick they won't have time to verify it."

Her father shook his head. "Do not do this, Bee. It's too dangerous."

"This human is willing to sacrifice herself for our people. Would you honestly ask less of me?"

Cassandra put the poor man out of his misery. "You don't look old enough to be ascending. One look at you and they'll know something's up. Plus if your queen was killed, they'll be on the lookout for you as well."

Tela leaned forward. "I'm the best option. They hate the unascended, but if I bring them you and Bejka, they might consider that I've proved myself enough to get another chance. They're all about survival of the strongest."

"This is our best chance of getting near the cave, my queen," Mathadar reluctantly agreed. "I can't imagine any other way because no one approaches the cave without approval from the queens."

"It sounds like a longshot to me. I don't want to risk Bejka. She's too young for a mission like this."

"Do not dare speak for me, human queen. I may be young but I am not weak. This is my time of proving and I will not have it stolen away by an alien queen who does not understand our ways."

Frowning at the youngster, Cassandra quipped, "I'm gonna remind you that you said that when you catch a laser burn trying to get away from those crazy parasites."

"Your anger does not stir quickly, human." The girl's father carefully chose his next words. "I will network with the elders and arrange for my daughter and you to be spirited away from whatever holding cell they place you in. I have no way of saving Tela because no males are allowed on the holy grounds around the cave."

Cassandra saw Pern slip in as they were talking. "With permission of the queens, I would like to secure the other human females and our young. We need them as far from this conflict as possible."

"That makes good sense. Take the reptilian vessel. No one from the fleet will think to stop a trade ship when we've taken two warships in battle, three including Tela's training vessel."

Mathadar spoke up again. "If it pleases the queens, I will interrogate the aquatics and force them to tell us the location of Earth. We will pick a rendezvous spot and all meet up for the final voyage."

"Though this is a good rough draft to work off of, we need to plan out a more detailed approach," Cassandra suggested.

Mathadar pulled up a planning document and they kicked around ideas for hours, arguing over every detail until a firm plan emerged.

21 EMPTY-HANDED

Though the warriors obsessed over the plan for days, planned out every detail, and came up with contingency plans, so much could still go wrong. He'd had so little time with the new queen, the thought of losing her paralyzed him with fear. Still, worrying into a stupor was not the way forward. He had to be alert and ready for danger instead of lost in his own thoughts.

Leaning over his computer console, he watched Tela's training ship heading for the surface of Dracon One. His home world provoked a mix of memories for him. After beating answers out of the aquatics over the last few days, he'd found out all about how they'd found a rupture in the fabric of space-time, allowing them to travel across the universe in a few lunars instead of the fifty or so solar revolutions. It was hidden in an asteroid field in a little-used part of their sector. That explained to Mathadar why it had not been discovered before now.

They were maintaining communications silence for mission integrity, according to their queen. Mathadar wasn't sure how familiar she was with military protocols, but he didn't argue with her over a statement such as this. His new queen put herself in danger to rescue her queen friend, Tela, and the hatchlings. Even now she was on her knees, bound with bruises covering her body. The bruises were compliments of his medical team who created them without injuring her. Still, seeing her marked in such a way pricked at his pride.

Gorok's voice sounded off over his shoulder. "What do you calculate their chances of surviving this mission are, Commander?"

Turning to face Bejka's sire, he felt his soul ache for this man. He'd committed the ultimate crime of killing his own queen. That was something that rarely happened. Breeders were not warriors. Mathadar had yet to learn the way of such a deed.

Turning his attention to the breeder's question, he thought it over for the hundredth time. "I believe that though the probability is low, they will beat the odds. We have to trust that Entares will watch out for her own. The goddess will never give us more than we can bear."

Nodding, Gorok dropped into a seat and sat staring at the view screen. "I wish that I could trade places with my Bejka. I would give my life a thousand times over to keep her safe."

"You have raised her well and killed to give her a chance at freedom of a life without the stain of a parasite corrupting her will. Now you must let her be the queen you raised her to be."

The breeder glanced at the bulge growing on Mathadar's side. "Your human queen hangs on your every word and looks to you first for counsel. I am pleased to see our warriors treated with the respect they deserve at long last. I hope to have your little spawn and mine train together one day."

Shocked, Mathadar dipped his head. "From your lips to the goddess' ear, my friend."

"Do you think there truly exists a sector of space where the queens and their parasites are not known?"

"My queen and the other human queens swear it is true. I have no reason to doubt them. I live for the day my spawn can run free on a planet with no parasites nor queens to crush them under her foot."

"Seeing my little one bound and subjugated wounded my soul."

"She chose her fate. I would hardly call her subjugated. She was giving the warriors instructions on how to best bind her hands. She will be a benevolent but exacting queen one day."

Another warrior spoke. "They have landed near the cave. The elders are relaying footage of their situation, but we have no sound."

"I never expected them to allow the defeated queens near the cave. It makes me wonder if they have some devious reason for doing so."

"What did the elders say about it?" Mathadar asked.

"They believe the priestesses wish to subject your human queen to the waters to see if the parasites will attach to her body as well."

"That seems much like something they would do."

The image on the huge view screen shifted to an overhead view of the mouth of the cave. Tela was dragging Cassandra and Bejka across a small flat grassy area and tossed them before three Draconian females with wrinkles covering their skin. Each had faded spots and drooping wings. The two bound females appeared appropriately cowed, though Mathadar doubted very much that they were.

Tela spoke to the older queens, gesturing between herself and the mouth of the cave. She thumped her chest and lifted her chin defiantly. The three priestesses spoke together for a few moments and one gestured toward the mouth of the cave.

Tela spun on her heel and headed for the opening. The older women began to talk again. Mathadar could see several more queens milling about. They were wearing gowns. He was surprised to discover none of them wore battle armor or carried more than a casual sidearm. Then he remembered that since this was a holy place, access to the area was controlled. They would have little need for a security force.

Cassandra tossed out a flash grenade. It exploded, neutralizing everyone in the vicinity except herself and Bejka, who were wearing shields tuned to the frequency of the grenade. They tore off their bindings that were applied more for show than restraint and headed for the cave.

~ Cassandra ~

Running into the cave with Bejka at her heels, Cassandra pulled the tiny queen weapon from her clothing. They found Tela searching around the cave, looking behind boulders and in two antechambers. The cave itself was rather primitive. It had images of sea monsters carved in stone upon the walls, glowing gel lamps strewn around, and three seats carved into nearby rocks, sized for a Draconian queen. Cassandra didn't have to think very long to decide who sat in those seats.

She trotted over to Tela. "We've got to hurry. They

probably picked up on the flash grenade. We've only got minutes to kill the creature and get the hell out of here."

Turning, she raced to the back of the cave. "Follow me. The water is this way."

The three of them came to a stop inside the doorway of the back chamber, gawking at a huge empty hole where the pool of water had clearly been. There were tiny luminescent larvae lying around the edges of the pool and some floating inside the now-shallow waters.

"She's gone," Cassandra gasped. "They've taken her away."

Bejka hissed. "Scorch the larvae and let's get out of here."

The three of women raised their queen weapons and laid waste to the remaining parasites. When they were finished there was nothing but black scorch marks on the floor of the cave. Running as fast as their legs would carry them, they exited the cave and took the path the elders had promised would lead to water. Finding the ocean, they dove in, stuck respirators in their mouths, and followed a long meandering path of coral to an underground cave. When they ducked under it and swam up, they broke the surface and were greeted by a group of elders. There were about a dozen of them, all breeders.

"Come, queens. Let us attend to your needs."

Cassandra allowed two of the elders to pull her up out of the water. "What the hell happened to the creature? The pool was empty."

"The priestesses were fearful that word had spread of the Vithacan queen. She is ancient and integral to their way of life. They tried to move her to a safer location off-world."

He handed her a large thick cloth and began to pull her clothing off. "This morning, there was a commotion in the great hall. Our sources report the queen mother's ship was raided and she was abducted by males with great horns wrapping around their heads. Their ship seemed to disappear in the blink of an eye. The priestesses were desperate for information. They sought to infect you so they could be certain the information you gave was truthful. Shall I assume you refused the few remaining parasites?"

Bejka nodded. "We made certain none of the vermin survived. Does that mean the rule of the queens will come to end?"

"I wish that were the case." Helping them into dry clothing, he continued. "I believe the queens will adapt. They propagate in one of two ways. One was the queen mother spawning. Those tiny spawn will never become fully grown because our queens do not live long enough for them to mature fully. We have known them to take a fist-sized sample from the Vithacan queen and place it inside one of our females. It grows and latches onto the host's brain stem."

"Why would they do something like that?"

"We have only recently been aware of the parasites and many Draconian males have given their lives so we might learn more about how they use our females. We work tirelessly to discover a way to defeat them. However, our communication between the home world and the ships is fractured. "

"Do you know why I didn't ascend?" Tela asked.

Once again the old man shook his head. "We do not know, Queen Teladora."

Cassandra thought it over for a bit. "Could she have some kind of natural immunity to the parasites?"

The talkative older man sighed. "It is possible. We know nothing for certain about the parasites."

"Maybe you should take biological samples from Tela and see if you can figure out what's going on there."

"We will, but now we must meet your males. If we do not hurry, they might be discovered before they can get you on board and lift off."

Cassandra couldn't get her head around the fact that they'd done the impossible but the Vithacan queen always seemed to be a step ahead of them. That led her to believe they had a traitor in their midst. Running through all the possibilities in her mind, she just couldn't imagine anyone doing something like that.

They were guided out through the back of the cave and down a rocky embankment on the other side of a mountain. There didn't seem to be anyone around for miles. Cassandra broke into a run when she saw her shuttle. The others were only a few steps behind her. Mathadar stepped out to meet her, capturing her in his arms. He didn't seem to be able to keep his hands off her. Perhaps he was checking to make sure she was okay. If so, she didn't mind.

"The creature was gone. They moved her and she ended up being abducted by some alien race nobody's seen before."

"May the goddess have mercy on their souls, for they know not what they have taken," Mathadar responded.

"If they aren't careful she'll destroy their entire society like she did ours," Tela said.

"Tela ain't wrong about that," Cassandra said.

"I don't know how much good killing off the few remaining parasites will be. It feels like a hollow victory."

The elder who helped them dress sighed. "You must make for the rift and get you and yours out of this sector."

Cassandra reached out and grasped the breeder's shoulder. "Come with us. You deserve to be free."

"We talked amongst ourselves and decided to stay. It's more important to pass along information and help others escape if we can."

Bejka spoke up quickly. "I command you all to accompany us to free space."

A ghost of a smile flickered on the elder's face before he answered. "Thank you for trying to force us to seek a better life for ourselves. However, we are intractable in our desire to stay for now. Do not worry over us. You may yet see us when our work here is done, my queen."

Stepping back, Mathadar and the other warriors drew them into the shuttle and it was in the air within moments, heading back to their ship. Mathadar wrapped her in his wings and ran his nose up and down the side of her face over and over again. He seemed anxious and kind of needy.

Cassandra cupped his face in her hands and gave him a nice long kiss. That calmed him in some ways and made him more anxious in others. Her hand drifted down to the two bulges on his hip. "Thanks for coming down to get me and thanks for the double trouble you're brewing in there. I can't wait to hold our hatchlings."

Mathadar smiled at her. "They're going to be a handful. Draconian young always are."

Cassandra realized something for the first time. No matter how complicated or dangerous things got, Mathadar always wrapped her in his wings and they shoved it all aside in favor of making time for each other. She really loved that about him. That brief mental respite often gave her the strength to get back up and do it all over again.

She felt them touch down in the loading bay and knew their special moment was coming to an end. Stealing one last quick kiss, she slid back off his lap and stood. When she turned around everyone was staring at them, everyone except Tela, who was similarly occupied with Trace.

No sooner did the bay doors close behind them than their ship turned and made for the rendezvous spot. She murmured, "I honestly need to sleep. Muscles ache that I didn't even know I had."

"We have time to sleep before we reach the rendezvous point. I will miss our tiny quarters when we are aboard your warship again."

She grinned. "It is kind of cozy in there." Since they were on Tela's ship, the main queen's chamber belonged to her and her breeders. That was just fine with Cassandra and Mathadar. Sometimes a small room with a big bed was just the ticket.

22 ONE WAY OUT

MATHADAR

After getting a full cycle of sleep, Mathadar sat in the captain's chair with his queen at his side. Was it cramped? Yes. Did he care? Absolutely not. His tail curled around her calf and his wing wrapped around her back. The need to have his hands on her after the dangerous mission had not subsided, and he worried that it never would. It was ten times worse now that the healers had verified she was carrying his child. Every time a being was brought aboard one of their ships, standard protocol was for them to be scanned for viruses and such. Her scan revealed a tiny cluster of cells growing in her womb. The healers report it can be only one thing: their unborn child.

"Are you okay, gorgeous? You seem a bit uptight."

Rather than notifying her of the healer's finding and screaming at her to never leave the ship again, he cleared his throat and answered his queen appropriately. "I am well, my queen. I just worry that the rift might have closed."

"We're coming up on it now."

A long slash in the darkness of space was visible on the view screen. It appeared to be a vertical even horizon shimmering in white, pinks, and purples. Since it was large enough for a battleship to break through, their smaller vessel should easily be able to fly thought the rift.

"I can't believe we found it. You're going to love the Naxis."

"Wherever you are is where I belong. Where are the other ships? They should have arrived before us."

"We're picking up three transponder signals on the other side, sir. It appears that they've already entered the anomaly," the navigator reported.

Cassandra took a deep breath. "Take us in when you're ready."

The navigational officer's hand flew over the console and the ship edged forward. "Do you mind if I ask why our Queen Teladora is not commanding her own ship this day, Queen Cassandra?"

"I heard someone came into her hormones a little early. I doubt you'll see her or Trace for days. We can't wait for her to come up for air, and I know she wouldn't want us to."

"This is a strange new experience for us, to ask questions of a queen and get truthful answers."

"What's your name?"

"I am Odem, Teladora's hatch mate."

"You look like your sister a bit when it comes to spots and coloring."

"Draconians are a colorful species, Queen Cassandra. We will be breaching the event horizon in ten, nine, eight, seven, six, five..."

Excitement strummed through Cassandra's chest as he counted down. She couldn't wait to exit the Exion. Just as they were crossing the threshold, a blast came out of nowhere and hit them in the rear.

"Unknown ship attacking. Shields are down to seventy-three percent and holding. A few more blasts like that and we're going to be in trouble."

"Accelerate, Odem. Get us out of their range."

"They're accelerating, my queen. I believe they mean to speed though the event horizon as well."

"Oh, hell no. Mathadar, can use your secret communications system to speak with the males on that ship? Get them to get rid of their queen. I hate to keep sticking them in escape pods, but we can't have one of them loose infecting all the females in our sector."

Mathadar rushed over to one of the consoles and worked with another warrior to make contact. After some rushed communication, he turned back to speak to her. "Their queen is on the bridge. The only way to get rid of her in any kind of timely fashion is to jettison the bridge section. It's designed to serve as a life pod, but they'll have to sacrifice their bridge crew."

"Tell them to make a run for the door and jettison the hub the moment they can separate. Tell them to save as many of the bridge crew as they can."

"We need to get out of their way. Once they separate, they'll be without power or guidance. When they slip through the anomaly, we'll need to lock on a tractor beam or grapple and tow them."

"Well, we definitely don't want them to drift. Get us through the event horizon and out of their way. Let them know we'll render any and all assistance on the other side."

"Are you certain, my queen? We know nothing of these males."

"We know they're Draconian and in need of assistance. That's all I need to know."

"It will be as you command."

Suddenly, everyone was moving at once. Mathadar did

his best to make sure everything went as planned. Unfortunately, the plan was always changing. Saving another thousand warriors was worth their time and trouble. The more warriors they had, the better position they would be in to defend a new home world.

When they blasted through to the Naxis, Mathadar knew his life had just changed for the better.

Odem carefully maneuvered them out of the way and turned on the rear scanners so they could see what was coming through the rift.

The ship came careening through the rift and it was clear someone else was firing at the other vessel.

Cassandra jumped to her feet. "What's going on?"

Mathadar stood behind her. "I believe another ship joined the battle. The enemy vessel is trying to destroy the ship rather than allow it to escape through the rift. With no navigation speak of nor weapons, they're an easy target."

"Fire back as best you can. Keep them off that beleaguered ship and be careful not to hit them. I don't think they can take many more direct strikes."

"Yes, my queen."

The weapons officer began a volley of surgical strikes through the rift and several struck their mark. Right after the ship slipped through, the bridge section came spinning through the rift, only now it was half the size it was before. Since the two ships were still firing at each other, the bridge module was caught in the crossfire. Suddenly, it exploded in a ball of white light.

Cassandra gasped, her hands flying to her throat. "Did we do that or did the enemy vessel?"

The weapons officer looked up from his console. "Neither. The queen initiated a self-destruct sequence."

"She sacrificed herself, but why? Maybe she wanted to

keep us out of Exion space? You have to admit that we tore the place up and attacked their holy place."

Mathadar didn't think that was the reason. "I believe they wished to protect the creature that was stolen away from being transported out of the Exion."

"If they don't know where she is or who took her, how do they know she hasn't slipped through already?"

Mathadar turned to his intelligent queen. "They likely have no knowledge of such things. They're just intent on closing off that option."

Dropping back down into the chair, Cassandra wrapped her arms around her waist. "Now we get organized. We need each ship to make a detailed list of its needs and resources. Focus on repairs to life support first, then on food supplies."

Mathadar sat beside her. "Does a queen's work never end, my sweet? It worries me that there is something going on every moment of every day. You should rest now."

Her head turned to look up at him. "Have you lost your mind? We've got several thousand people to care for and many young. Now's not the time to go lie down."

He reached out and pressed one large hand over her still-flat belly. "I'm afraid that I must insist, my queen. The others can send us reports in our quarters. You must pick a warship and we will make a nest for our young."

Her hands came up to cover his. "Are you saying what I think you're saying?"

"You and I are with young. We have given ourselves freely to the cause of freedom for these people. Now, we slow down and care for ourselves and our little spawn. No one would fault you for this."

"Who's going to be on the bridge?"

"We have many competent warriors. They can train the

new queens to take shifts. Though they are still few, we do have queens wishing to render assistance. I say we allow them to do just that. They can handle the day-to-day operations and you will supervise, making appearances when necessary."

Chewing her bottom lip, it was clear his pretty queen was still getting her head around being with child—his child.

"I suppose it doesn't matter where I work," she finally responded quietly.

"Are you pleased to be breeding?" He posed the question, because she seemed lost in her own thoughts.

Her lovely face lit up in an instant and her arms came up around his neck. She didn't see just the plain warrior that Mathadar was. She made the mating gesture and his chest swelled with a kind of pride he honestly never knew existed.

"We're going to have a real family, with three whole babies."

"It's actually two hatchlings and a human baby," he said.

"Count them. Three kids for you and me. It's gonna be fantastic."

"Do you think the one in your belly will be born with wings?"

Smiling fondly at him, she teased, "Humans don't carry babies in our bellies. That's where our food goes. We have a special organ for that. It's called a womb. Wings? Gosh, I hope so. I don't want him or her to feel left out."

He stood and scooped up his lovely queen into his arms and headed for the door. He did not like the longing looks the other warriors had when looking upon her lovely face or her beautiful body. The thought of her growing large with his child pulled out every possessive instinct he had. They would never stop staring when she was round with child.

Suddenly, a thought popped into his head. "Do humans incubate their young?"

She shook her head. "Not unless they're born early and they're not fully developed."

Leaning down to kiss her pretty soft hair, Mathadar murmured, "If she does not have wings, we will have no need to leash her."

"Say what? We are not leashing our kids, big guy. That's a hard no from me."

"Then you are fine if the wind blows them away or if they fly away and get lost?"

"Well no, I'm definitely not okay with that."

"I was chained as a hatchling. I still have the scarring around my ankles because of it. We will use something soft that does not tear their skin."

His queen began to tear up. "I really love you."

"I like this human love word. I human love you as well, my queen."

"Do you think you'll ever get to the point where you feel comfortable calling me by my name? Since I'm carrying your child, being on a first-name basis would make things less weird."

Strolling into their small room, he sat her on the bed. Squatting down, he looked deeply into her eyes. "I do not like this word, 'weird.'" Gesturing between the two of them, he insisted, "We are not weird together. You are my queen and I am your Takadon. Nothing about that is weird."

"Okay, what's the translation program showing you for the word 'weird'?"

"I am getting images of people with small heads and big

bodies, small dogs being carried in a small decorative bag by a queen wearing very little clothing, and ..."

Holding up one hand, his queen cut him off. "Forget all that stuff. Weird can also just mean unusual. Where I come from males call their wives by their names."

"The other warriors would see that as a sign of disrespect."

Reaching out to run a hand over one of his horns, she asked sweetly, "Can you at least use my name when we are alone?"

"I do not know how I feel about that." If it were any other queen asking such a thing, Mathadar would suspect it to be a test of his honor. However, he knew his queen would never do such a thing.

Her voice turned soft and she purred in his ear, "I think it's really sexy when you say my name. You do that every now and then when we're making love."

Running his tongue over his bottom lip, he responded quietly, "This I already know. Your cunt tightens around my cock when I say your name."

"Well, can you really blame me? You have a sexy voice and a really nice cock."

She complimented him all the time. He didn't know why but this time he felt it more profoundly. Running his nose up one side of her face and down the other, he whispered, "My Cassandra, how could I deny you anything? You're my entire world."

"That's ten kinds of sweet. How's about we pick up with that reverse-revidian thingy?"

"I almost hesitate to attempt it again. It seems that every time we are in position, our ship gets attacked or some other crisis comes up."

"You wouldn't deny your queen a taste of your body would you, my king?"

Shock tore through his chest and he felt his mouth go dry.

"The translation program embedded at the base of my skull is sending images to my brain of two richly dressed beings, a male and a female. They are sitting in oversized chairs and ruling over their people hand-in-hand with shiny metal ornamental objects set on top of their heads. They smile at each other and nothing can come between them. Their little ones have small bits of metal on their heads as well, both the males and the females. They are treated equally by their parental units.'

This was the moment he truly understood what he meant to his precious queen. She respected him and wished him to share power with her. She would bestow love equally upon their little ones, no matter if they were queens or warriors. Of course his brain knew all this, but somehow now his heart truly believed it. Never had he felt such joy in his mind and body. His spirit soared because his queen lifted him up, just as he did for her.

Like the king in the images, he brought her hand to his mouth and bestowed a human kiss on the back of it. She had no bit of metal around her finger like the image the translation program sent, so he vowed to create one for her. Once he did that, their lives would be perfect, like in the image.

"So that's a yes to the reverse-revidian?"

She moved the tiny hairs above her eyes as she spoke. Most beings would find hairs on one's eyes to be off-putting, but his queen's tiny hairs are lovely.

"You may do with me as you please, my Cassandra. I am yours in every conceivable way."

"Keep that up and you're going to have me churning out sexy games for us to play again."

His nostrils flared at the reminder of when she touched herself while he watched. He wanted that and everything else his naughty queen had to offer. He thought of flipping her over and mounting her from behind all the time. As he rubbed his chin, he thought that perhaps she might like his newest perversion. They were both smart and capable beings. It made him think they wouldn't run out of creative ideas for a very long time.

ELEVEN MONTHS LATER

CASSANDRA

Watching the little ones playing out the window, Cassandra realized how very necessary leashes turned out to be, especially for toddlers with wings. Tela even leashed her little ones, even though she had wings and could fly after them. Then again, when you had a dozen or more, it was just a numbers thing.

Mathadar stopped by and stared at Cassandra breastfeeding their daughter. He normally loved watching her breastfeed, but today he was frowning.

"What's wrong, Math? You don't seem happy."

Gesturing toward their little one with one hand, he shook his head. "She's doing it again."

"What, babe?"

"Sleeping. She does it often and for long periods of time, only to wake, eat, and go back to doing it some more. Our sons seem worried and to be honest, so am I. Is all this sleeping normal for a mostly-human baby?"

Cassandra pulled the baby off her chest. Mathadar burped the little princess as he walked around with her on his shoulder. She was drowsy already. Fixing her clothing, Cassandra tried to be reassuring.

"Human newborns sleep like it's their freaking job. Don't worry, babe. She'll be up and getting into everything sooner than you think. In no time at all, she'll be giving the boys a run for their money."

"I am learning all your human expressions, though most of them make very little sense."

"Like Draconian expressions make any sense at all. For instance, Pharon told the boys to rip a claw. What in the world does that even mean?"

"He's reminding them to keep their claws sharp. In olden times we ripped our claws on stones to sharpen them. Sharp claws are safe claws."

"Yep, I don't know what that means either."

Placing their little one in the perpetual rocking cradle that looked suspiciously like a cage, he closed the top. It was made of woven sticks and designed to keep tiny beings with wings from flying off. "The breeders are caring for our young this day, my Cassie. What do you wish to do with your day? We can inspect the building going on in the city if you like or enjoy a swim in the lagoon."

"How's about we take a little nap together? Things could turn sexy."

"Let us enjoy the lagoon and see if sexy things happen there."

"I can never say no to you. You always get your way with me," she said.

"You must be mixing me up with one of your other mates. I am the long-suffering male who barely gets to spend time with his mate because she always has a child in her lap."

Grabbing her towel and pulling on her swimsuit, she

teased him mercilessly. "Are you jealous of your own children, Math? That's not okay. You do know that, right?"

"Right or wrong, I wish you in my lap more often. You can even bring a little one if you like."

"That's real generous of you, babe. I'll have to think about it and get back to you."

Snaking an arm around her waist, he tugged her back and under his wing. "There will be no thinking it over. I am your king and you will obey my every word."

Cassandra couldn't hold it in anymore and burst out laughing. "You're a real hoot these days. What's gotten into you anyway?"

"You may ask me that when I put you on your knees to pleasure me beside the lagoon."

Grinning like a mad fool, she continued joking around with him. "I'm really warming up to this lagoon idea. Are we walking or flying?"

"Flying," he responded curtly. "It's faster."

When he lifted her into his arms, it took him only a moment to launch his massive body into the air. She loved seeing their new home world from high in the sky.

The breeze blew through her hair and a pale sun warmed her face. A large bird circled around them, having a look. The avian's face was strangely compelling. He squawked before flying away. The landscape was untouched, and the planet's resources included precious minerals and gemstones. There was an abundance of fresh water, and the soil was perfect for cultivating crops. In short, they couldn't have asked for a better planet.

Mathadar landed on the ground beside their special lagoon and set her down gently on her feet. Stepping forward, he wrapped both wings around her and pulled her in for a kiss. That was his secret weapon for getting his sexy way with her. His talented tongue liked to dance all around her favorite spots and no woman could resist that kind of seduction.

Cassandra enjoyed his sexy lips far too much before stepping back and pulling off the top of her swimsuit. His nostrils flared in that sexy way she loved when she sank to her knees. His naked chest always made her hot. When he stepped forward, one hand dropped to pull his pants down in the front. He was already sporting a huge boner. It would be fun to watch him lose control.

Taking him in her hands, she stroked him a couple of times before he tangled his hand into her hair and encouraged her do what they both loved. Running her tongue over him always caused his wings to unfurl and his horns to slide back against his head. This time was no different. His tail snaked between her legs and dipped into her swimsuit bottoms. The man could do some nasty stuff with that tail, stuff that left her a quivering mess on the ground.

Suddenly he lifted her from the ground and lifted her up with his wings. Balancing her bottom on his hands, he began to explore her body with his devilish tongue. He took his time teasing her and making her beg for release before he slid her down his body and right onto his gigantic cock. His wings flapped and they lifted off the ground with her legs locked around his hips and him still working himself in and out of her body like there was no tomorrow.

Midair sex beat every other kind hands down in her opinion. Mathadar once said he never felt freer than when he was flying, so she suspected this was his favorite as well. Those rings were the tough part. If it weren't for those rubbing all the hot spots inside her body, she could probably last a heck of a lot longer. As it stood, she was clenching down around his cock within fifteen minutes.

It was too soon for her lusty warrior. He'd spent the last eleven months making up for all the really dirty sex he never got before they met. That came in real handy when the pregnancy hormones were flooding her system.

He stilled inside her body to give his love a moment to recover. Never one to miss a chance to tease him, she leaned over and ran her tongue over his nipple. That was what finally pushed him right over the edge.

The next thing she knew he was pulling out and they were on the ground with him turning her on all fours in the soft grass. Her guy loved this position as well because it put him squarely in charge. Maybe he had a few control issues, but she loved giving it up for him, so it was all good.

It was kind of cute how he tried to be all cool and gentle, but three strokes in and he was fucking her like he couldn't ever get enough. She was wet enough to take him though, and somewhere in the middle of all that, Cassandra realized his mating scent had released again.

The thought of him breeding for her again flipped all the right switches and she began pushing back against him, wanting more and harder and faster. She felt his tail between her legs, searching for her clit and tickling everything it touched. When it speared the tight rosette of her ass, she knew he was being extra dirty because his breeding hormones were getting the better of him. That just made it worse.

One large hand landed on her shoulder and he pulled her back into a sitting position, still moving inside her. His mouth moved to her throat and his deep sexy voice sounded in her ear. "When we're together like this, tell me, my sweet sexy little queen, who is breeding whom."

When he reached around to play with her nipples, Cassandra could no longer think rationally, much less make words. There was nothing but the feel of his body moving against hers and the burning need to experience the kind of bliss that only her Takadon could deliver. His other hand drifted down to tease her clit and he pinched her nipple, twisting it. Cassandra fell apart in his arms, knowing nothing in the universe could compare to their new life.

Mathadar milked every bit of pleasure he could for her from their lovemaking, and her orgasm seemed to last for an endless eternity. Leaning back against his hard chest, Cassandra caught her breath as he blasted hot jets of his seed into her body.

Turning her face to look at him, he ran his nose down the side of her face. His kisses were smoking hot; it was this tender gesture of affection that was so often used by his people that touched her heart. It was how she knew her battered warrior loved her the same way she loved him. Though he had wings and claws, he was her idea of perfect.

THE END

READY FOR MORE SEXY Draconian adventures? Read *Alien Protector's Rescued Bride (Draconian Warriors Book 5)* now!

GLOSSARY

Akes – Draconian god of hunting, war and violence. He is the consort to Entares, the benevolent goddess worshiped by Draconian males.

Antar – Right (Lutar is left.)

Avada – Small carrot like vegetable that is seasoned and wrapped in a dry leaf.

Challenge –Draconian queens settle disagreements and property disputes by challenging one another in single combat. It is usually a battle to the death.

Clade – Group of Draconians who are descended from a common set of genetic code.

Dark Star – Another term from black hole.

Doma – Type of Draconian flatbread.

Dracon Two – The name the second wave of Draconian warriors nicknamed their new home world. Dracon Two's real name is Onello. It is located in Naxis space. The planet was originally named by Queen Cassandra after a Greek god. It was unofficially renamed Dracon Two because the name their new queen chose is very near the word for feces in the Draconian tongue.

Draconian - Species created by mixing dragon DNA with humanoid DNA. There are many family lines with unique strengths and weaknesses.

Entares – Draconian goddess of beauty, peace and joy. The males worship her as she represents their desire for females to show kindness and respect to them for their many sacrifices, rather than the harsh treatment they normally receive.

Entaza – Dish eaten with the living larva still wiggling in the dish. Common food in Exion space.

Exion – Vast Sector of space encompassing the Draconian home world. Exion is ruled by a race of ruthless females bent on conquest and power.

Hatching – Draconian method of reproduction by which warriors conceive and carry eggs.

Hatchling – Noun: Child. Hatching is a verb: Act of creating young by a male Draconian. Males hatch many times during their lifetimes.

Hatch Mate – Refers to only the children hatched during the same cycle of breeding.

Laser Pistol –A weapon used in battles and self-defense which uses power packs to fire short laser bursts.

Lunar – Equivalent of a complete phase of the primary moon traveling around Dracon One. This is a standard unit of measurement used by many space faring species, even when not on their home planets.

Lutar - Left. (Antar is Right)

Maradox – Queen Rovanda's ship, which was boarded and taken by Queen Cassandra and Mathadar.

Moltan – Malevolent aliens who attack and destroy other vessels.

Naxis – Vast sector of space encompassing five galaxies, including the Milky Way.

Obsidian – The name of a Draconian ship.

Parsec – Unit of distance. Used mostly in determining distance in space.

Parthenogenesis – Draconians males undergo parthenogenesis when exposed to a female's pheromones. It results them incubating eggs in their bodies which are released into specially designed incubators.

Phase Grenade – Device that sticks to the hull of a ship and disables their weapons.

Revidian – The word used by Draconians to denote a warrior performing oral sex on a queen.

Scion – A word used for offspring, no matter the age.

Solar Revolution – Equivalent of a complete revolution of Dracon One around its sun. This is a standard unit of measurement used by many space faring species, even when not on their home planets.

Strador Five – Planet populated by amphibians who discovered Earth and decided to abduct human women to sell on the open marketplace.

Strovian – Race of warriors who are at peace with the Draconians in the Naxis sector.

Tarken – Powerfully addicting drug used by queens in the Exion.

Takadon – The Draconian word for a male who is chosen to be the queen's primary breeder. He is to stay at her side constantly and is her protector.

Taladar – Species who initiated a trade agreement with Earth to exchange much-needed food and other supplies for human brides.

Tankea – Draconian word meaning love between a parent and child or between siblings.

Unders – Anything worn under one's uniform or regular clothing.

Tricon – Unit of thickness.

Utaka Larva – Pupa stage of growth for tiny colorful flying creatures the Draconians keep for pets.

Vithacan – Symbionts that attach themselves to other creatures and survive off their emotional energy. Soul-suckers is a disrespectful term for their race.

Zelerians – Race of squid-like creatures with few humanoid features.